While Lance was contemplating his next move, Caroline held his cheeks and pulled his face down to hers, whereby she kissed him.

It lingered intoxicatingly for a long moment before she pulled back, gazed into his eyes and asked boldly, "Is that what you were waiting to do?"

"Yeah." He blushed. "I have to be sure to add mind reader to your many charming qualities."

She laughed. "Go for it. But I have to admit, it was less about having a sixth sense than it was your body language."

"Oh, really?" Was it that obvious? He couldn't deny that she did things to him that his body couldn't help but react to. In spite of that, Lance tried not to embarrass himself again.

"Figured we may as well get that sexual tension between us over with," she said teasingly as she unlocked her car. "Now we can get back to business. See you later, Detective Warner."

HONOLULU COLD HOMICIDE

R. BARRI FLOWERS

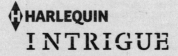

In memory of my beloved mother, Marjah Aljean, a devoted
longtime fan of Harlequin romances, who inspired me to do my
best in finding success in my professional and personal lives.
To H. Loraine, the true love of my life, whose support has been
unwavering through the many years together, and to the loyal fans
of my romance, mystery, suspense and thriller fiction published
over the years. Lastly, a nod goes out to super editors Allison
Lyons and Denise Zaza for the opportunity to lend my literary
voice and creative spirit to the Harlequin Intrigue line.

HARLEQUIN®
INTRIGUE™

Recycling programs
for this product may
not exist in your area.

ISBN-13: 978-1-335-58244-7

Honolulu Cold Homicide

Copyright © 2023 by R. Barri Flowers

For questions and comments about the quality of this book,
please contact us at CustomerService@Harlequin.com.

Harlequin Enterprises ULC
22 Adelaide St. West, 41st Floor
Toronto, Ontario M5H 4E3, Canada
www.Harlequin.com

Printed in U.S.A.

R. Barri Flowers is an award-winning author of crime, thriller, mystery and romance fiction featuring three-dimensional protagonists, riveting plots, unexpected twists and turns, and heart-pounding climaxes. With an expertise in true crime, serial killers and characterizing dangerous offenders, he is perfectly suited for the Harlequin Intrigue line. Chemistry and conflict between the hero and heroine, attention to detail and incorporating the very latest advances in criminal investigations are the cornerstones of his romantic suspense fiction. Discover more on popular social networks and Wikipedia.

Books by R. Barri Flowers

Harlequin Intrigue

Hawaii CI

The Big Island Killer
Captured on Kauai
Honolulu Cold Homicide

Chasing the Violet Killer

Visit the Author Profile page at Harlequin.com.

CAST OF CHARACTERS

Lance Warner—A detective sergeant with the Honolulu PD's Criminal Investigation Division. When a homicide case seems eerily similar to the murder of his sister Bonnie two decades ago, Lance teams up with the cold case detective he ended things with six months ago to track down her killer. Will the flames between them reignite in the process?

Caroline Yashima—A cold case investigator for the Hawaii Department of the Attorney General's Criminal Justice Division. Can she solve a twenty-year-old murder mystery and win back the victim's detective brother, whom Caroline has never gotten out of her system?

Roger Nielsen—A retired homicide detective who was the lead investigator in the Bonnie Warner murder. Was the investigation strictly by the book? Or does he have something to hide?

Dorian Powell—A Honolulu PD lieutenant who worked on the original murder case and has been haunted by it ever since. Does he have ulterior motives for wanting to reopen the cold case?

Kirsten Breckenridge—A onetime drug addict who threatened Bonnie the day before she died. Did she follow through on this in spite of an alibi and pick up where she left off twenty years later?

Shelley Pacheco—Bonnie's best friend. Does she remember something that can crack the cold case?

The Belt Strangler—Is murdering young women in Honolulu with the same MO as a cold case killer. Are they one and the same? Or is a copycat killer on the loose in paradise?

Prologue

Bonnie Warner fumbled with her keys as she stood at the door of her furnished ninth-floor apartment on Hawaii Kai Drive in Honolulu, on Oahu, the third-largest of the Hawaiian Islands and most populated. Oahu was often referred to as "The Gathering Place," and much of its population lived in Honolulu, the capital of Hawaii. Bonnie considered this both a blessing, with all the hustle and bustle, and a curse for the same reason. Overall, though, she saw it as a blessing, as there were so many wonderful things to see and do and friends to hang out with.

But for the moment, she would settle for getting inside the place she called home. It probably didn't help her cause that she was also trying to juggle a bag filled with microwave dishes, drinks and snacks, all typical fare for a just-turned twenty-four-year-old graduate student at the University of Hawai'i at Mānoa. Determined to complete the task without having to set the bag down, she managed to finally unlock the door and step inside the two-bedroom, one-bath unit that she had been renting for the past six months. Ever since she and Bradley broke up and, as a result, stopped living together. It was times like this that Bonnie wondered if it had been a mistake to end the relationship and go it alone, paying rent with limited income and savings as an admittedly dirt-poor student in a high-priced city. But what other choice was there? Hadn't he admitted to cheating on her with another student and was less than apologetic about it, as though it was her fault and not his, which told her he couldn't be trusted? The same was true with another man she had mistakenly gone out on a few dates with, only to find out that he was married and just looking for some action on the side. She wondered if she could ever trust any man, whatever his circumstances were, when there were so many attractive, sexy and willing women around for them to choose from or rotate between.

Bonnie waved off any regrets, knowing she'd done the right thing, as she walked across the porcelain flooring in a spaghetti strap tank top and formfitting patchwork jeans on her tall and slender physique. She could hear the crackling sounds of her new high-heeled thong sandals, bought for the fall semester, and hoped they were fully broken in at least by the start of the New Year in just over three months. After kicking them off, leaving her barefoot, she entered the tiny kitchen and put everything away, then poured herself a glass of red wine.

Bonnie truly missed her family back in St. Louis, Missouri, even though they encouraged her to pursue her doctorate degree in marine biology in Hawaii, so far away. She especially missed her little brother, Lance. Well, maybe not so little at six-two and with more than enough muscles spread across his hard body at just seventeen years old. In spite of their seven-year age difference, they were still pretty close as siblings. He was planning to visit next summer and she looked forward to teaching him to surf and more, while imagining he would have to fight off the sex-crazed teenage Hawaiian and vacationing girls.

Taking the wine with her, Bonnie headed for the master suite. All she could think of at the moment was relaxing in a nice hot bath. She went into the bathroom and cut on the water, then went back into the bedroom, where she turned on the ceiling fan out of habit and tied atop her head her long naturally blond hair, which everyone said was a perfect match for her bold blue eyes. She wasn't about to argue the point. After the bath, she hoped to study for a couple of hours and then decide what to do next to complete her day.

Before she could remove her clothes, Bonnie thought she heard a sound coming from the living room area. Was it her imagination? She had locked the front door, hadn't she? Cautiously, she moved out of the bedroom, peeked around the corner of the small apartment and saw no one. She breathed a sigh of relief. False alarm. As it was, she had not personally encountered any criminal activity since moving to Honolulu a year and a half earlier. Not including the standard vandalism and unruly behavior on campus from time to time by students. Still, knowing that Honolulu, like any big city, had its fair share of serious crimes, such as home invasions and burglaries, Bonnie found herself heading to the door to make sure it was actually locked.

It was only when she realized she had forgotten to lock it with the groceries in hand that Bonnie's heart skipped a beat and she wondered if someone could actually have entered the apartment. Had that been the case, wouldn't she have seen the person, since there was really nowhere to hide? She locked the door and hooked the door chain as an added precautionary measure. Before she could let down her guard, Bonnie heard a sound again and realized it was right behind her. Jerking her head around, she stared straight up into the cold, dark eyes of someone she recognized, who glared back at her as if on a mission to finish something that had never started. In a desperate bid to escape the menace, she turned her head and tried to unlock the door, realizing she had inadvertently become trapped in a nightmare from which there might be no escape.

When a long black leather belt was suddenly

wrapped around her neck, Bonnie found herself gasping for air. But the more she tried, the more constricted her airway became as the belt tightened around her slender neck, her assailant using strength and determination to shake off her valiant attempts to fight back and break free. Just before everything went black, Bonnie could only wonder what might have been had her promising life not been so cruelly taken away from her without just cause.

Chapter One

Caroline Yashima sat at her ergonomic workstation, where for the past seven months she had been kept busy as a cold case investigator for the Hawaii Department of the Attorney General, Criminal Justice Division. Before that, she worked for the CJD investigating environmental crimes, elder abuse, and Medicaid fraud and cases. Admittedly, she found her niche as a detective in the solving of cold homicide crimes that, if not swept under the rug, were more often than not forgotten over time by everyone other than loved ones. She should know. As a Japanese American, she was born two years after her parents immigrated to Honolulu, Hawaii, from Japan, where her uncle had been murdered in its capital city of Tokyo. The yakuza, an organized crime syndicate, had killed him for not capitulating to their demands that his restaurant be used for funneling illicit drugs. The killers had never been brought to justice.

Now thirty-four, with both parents dead from

natural causes, Caroline only wished she had gotten the chance to know her mother's brother, Ichiro.
But it was never to be. If she could give other victims of cold cases closure, then it was worth taking
on these often-challenging assignments. In her last
closed case, she had solved the forty-year-old murder
of a county prosecutor named Harvey Nakao, who
was shot to death while in his BMW in Kapiolani
Park in Honolulu. Turned out he was killed by an
errant bullet in a drug deal gone bad. The fact that
the culprit, identified through DNA as a drug traf-
ficker named Chauncey Duldulao, was also dead,
murdered while he was doing federal time in Cali-
fornia for another killing, didn't make the triumph
any less satisfying.

*At least I was able to offer Harvey's widow peace
of mind on some level*, Caroline thought, sitting back
in her mesh chair. The height had been adjusted to
account for her short legs and slender frame. As
usual when on duty, she kept her long brunette hair
in a chignon and, thus far, thankfully did not need
reading glasses for her big brown eyes. She was just
about to log on to her laptop when Caroline noticed
her boss entering the small, minimally furnished office with a double-hung window.

As administrator of the Criminal Justice Division,
Vera Miyasato was fifty years old and medium-sized
in her standard dark pleated pantsuit. She had gray
hair that was short and cropped, which went well

with a round face and sable-colored eyes. Caroline
tried to read her mind, but as usual, Vera managed
to keep her in the dark for as long as she wanted,
as if to aggravate her just for the sake of it. Holding
a folder up to her chest, Vera said in an even tone,
"Got a new case for you, Caroline."

"I have two cold cases still pending," she reminded
her, thinking about the unsolved murders of each
and the sometimes-painful process involved in investigating.

"It's called multitasking," Vera said with a dead-
pan look. "We all learn to live with it."

Caroline smiled dryly, having understood just
what she was getting herself into when she'd signed
up for the job. "In that case, I can hardly wait to jump
right into it." Was she really that eager to pour herself
into yet another assignment as a single woman with
no serious prospects at the moment? Since when did
becoming a workaholic act as a substitute for male
companionship?

"Glad to hear that." Vera seemed oblivious to her
personal crisis, dumping the folder on her desk. "This
one comes as a favor to a colleague and friend of
mine, Lieutenant Dorian Powell of the Honolulu Police Department's Criminal Investigation Division,"
she pointed out matter-of-factly. "It involves an unsolved case he worked on twenty years ago, where
a twenty-four-year-old female victim named Bonnie Warner was strangled to death in her Honolulu

apartment by an unknown assailant. Dorian thought a fresh set of eyes might be in order to tackle this one, which apparently bears some similarities to a ligature-strangulation homicide that was perpetrated in the city last night."

Caroline had heard about the latest murder, having picked it up on the news this morning before driving to work. The victim, Jill Hussey, had been discovered by her roommate in their apartment in Ewa Beach, a suburb of Honolulu. But at the moment, Caroline was much more tuned in to the name of the cold case victim. *Bonnie Warner*. It caused a reaction in her, as much for the deceased as for a living relative of Bonnie's whom Caroline had once been romantically involved with before it had ended on a sour note. "I'm somewhat familiar with Ms. Warner's case." She spoke in a subdued tone.

"Do tell?" Vera trained wide eyes on her with curiosity.

"I know—knew—her brother, Detective Sergeant Lance Warner. We crossed paths a while back during a case," Caroline said simply, knowing it went much further than that. But she saw no need to elaborate, as it wasn't relevant to the current situation. "Lance mentioned he'd lost his sister, Bonnie, years ago when she was a grad student on the island."

Vera considered this as she smoothed a wrinkle in her high-waisted pocketed pants. "I'm glad you two are already acquainted," she said with a catch to her voice. "You'll be working alongside Detective Warner, who is the lead investigator in the latest homicide case, while staying in your own lanes when necessary or prudent. The HPD Cold Case Unit will also be available for anything you need as it relates to this cold case."

Caroline nodded musingly, stung by the notion of having to work with the man who broke her heart two and half years ago. Would it be as awkward for him as for her? Or no big deal, as water under the bridge and time to let go of any lingering bad feelings? She responded as expected. "I'll take a look at the file and go from there."

Vera gave her a pleased look. "Hope you can achieve the same results you did in closing out the Harvey Nakao case," she said. "And put Detective Warner's mind to rest in solving his sister's murder, whether it's connected to the current murder investigation or not."

"Me too." Caroline wondered again if it was possible to work closely with Lance while maintaining a safe emotional detachment at the same time. Did she really have a choice? She had to woman up and be the skilled cold case detective she was, for better or worse.

"I'll let you get to it."

Caroline watched her leave before sitting back and staring out the window and reminiscing. It seemed like only yesterday that she first laid eyes on Lance

Warner. She was instantly drawn to his dark-haired, blue-eyed good looks. Not to mention his all-male tall and sturdy, long-legged build that was hard not to notice. They seemed to hit it off right away. Or so she thought. Putting aside his occasional moodiness and obvious pain from losing his sister seventeen years earlier, or even being in sometimes competing or overlapping law enforcement professions, Caroline had truly believed they could have a future together. Even marriage and children seemed possible down the line. Along with traveling the world together and enjoying the sights and sounds and each other's company, whenever the opportunity presented itself.

Then everything she had hoped for in their six-month relationship that came with falling in love crashed to a halt. Without adequate explanation—not to her, anyway—Lance pulled the proverbial rug out from beneath her. Whether it was merely a matter of cold feet, a fear of commitment or something else, he unceremoniously ended things between them and that was it. She never got a say in it. He decided it was over with no input from her. How fair was that? Caroline bit her thin lower lip out of a frustration she realized had never truly gone away, even after nearly three years of trying hard to put it behind her and regain equilibrium. For the most part, she had succeeded, able to keep her disillusion with relationships in check while pouring herself into work.

Now she was expected to work with Lance, whom

she had managed to avoid running into ever since
they broke up, in spite of both being in local law enforcement. Was this his doing? Or was he just as ten-
tative in reconnecting, even on a professional level?
Whatever the case, Caroline was committed to doing
her job, as always, and needed to keep her personal
issues with Lance on the back burner, no matter how
difficult. In this instance, the task at hand was to
find out who murdered Bonnie Warner and if the
unknown suspect or unsub was, indeed, up to his or
her old deadly tricks again.

Caroline opened up the folder and took a cursory
glance at the information. Bonnie Helene Warner,
age twenty-four. Born in St. Louis, Missouri, to parents Kevin and Loretta Warner, Bonnie had one sibling, Lance Troy Warner, then seventeen years of age.
The decedent was a doctoral student at the University of Hawai'i at Mānoa majoring in marine biology.

Caroline felt an immediate kinship beyond the
obvious, as she too had attended UH Mānoa, though
American studies was her major, with a minor in
sociology. She lifted a photograph of Bonnie Warner. *She was really pretty*, Caroline thought while
admiring the deep blue eyes and rich yellow-blond
hair with parted bangs. Lance bore a strong resemblance to his sister, albeit as a decidedly masculine,
square-jawed version of her with dark brown hair.

It gave Caroline a chill in imagining what it must
be like to lose a sibling. And at such a young age as

Lance was at the time. Had this sense of loss kept him from moving forward and into a steady and loving relationship? Or was she trying to justify being dumped by a man who Caroline thought had real feelings for her but apparently only cared for the hot sex between them and friendship with benefits? She looked at a crime scene photograph of Bonnie and saw that she was fully clothed and barefoot, lying on the floor of her apartment. Had she known her killer, with no indication of forced entry? Or had the killer known her, as opposed to being a total stranger?

Pushing aside the unsettling thoughts, Caroline took a quick look at the autopsy report. According to it, Bonnie Warner's death was ruled a homicide, with the official cause asphyxia resulting from ligature strangulation. The disturbing marks around the neck suggested that the murder weapon was a belt. There was no sign of a sexual assault, for which Caroline took some solace, hating the thought of Lance's sister being further victimized in that way. Could the unsub be a female? Women were certainly as capable as men of committing murder when motivated enough, including when motivated for sexual reasons. Or was the killer, male or female, driven by something else that was personal? Whatever the culprit's gender, Bonnie had still been deprived of living a long and meaningful life, which lay squarely on the shoulders of her killer. And for this Caroline would do her best to try to make sure the unsub, if still alive, was held accountable for both the victim and her brother.

With that thought in mind, Caroline left the office with a new sense of determination, even as she dreaded having to face Lance again in the process of working toward a common goal on a professional level. As for the history between them, she had to put that aside for now. Or was that asking too much, considering the way they left things?

Stepping outside, Caroline breathed in the warm, humid morning air in late September, as she stood in comfortable moc-toe loafers with ankle pants and a short-sleeved knit polo sweater. She made her way to an assigned parking spot for her department-issued vehicle, a red Toyota Camry. Once inside and seat belt on, Caroline took the five-minute drive from Queen Street, where the Department of the Attorney General was located, to the Honolulu Police Department on South Beretania Street. She took an extra moment to gather herself and then left the comfort of the car for a meeting with the detective that she hoped would help solve a twenty-year-old murder mystery.

DETECTIVE SERGEANT LANCE WARNER of the Honolulu Police Department's Criminal Investigation Division found it damned near impossible to look at the latest murder under his watch as run of the mill, where it concerned homicides in the city. Jill Hussey was twenty-four, the same way-too-young age his sister, Bonnie, was when she was killed, almost two decades ago. Like her, Jill was also the victim of an apparent ligature strangulation in her apartment at night. She even looked like Bonnie, Lance couldn't help but think as he regarded the slender decedent as she lay on a table in the morgue where the autopsy was underway at the Department of the Medical Examiner Building. With her attractive heart-shaped face surrounded by mounds of blond hair styled in a wavy shag, it pained him to see her life snuffed out like a candle. As had been the case with Bonnie. The notion that the two murders could actually be connected, ridiculous as it seemed, was even more unsettling to Lance.

Jill Hussey was an international flight attendant who had, according to Aimee Browning, her roommate, just returned to Honolulu from Tokyo when an unknown assailant either was invited or forced their way into the victim's apartment and attacked Jill. The unsub got away and had apparently taken one of the dress bootees with block heels that the decedent was wearing, but had left the victim's airline uniform intact. This oddity was not lost on Lance. He knew that one of the thong sandals Bonnie had worn the day she died had been stolen too by her killer and had never been recovered. Was this coincidence? Or had the perp resurfaced after two decades, only to set their sights on another young woman as if time had stood still? Though the latter seemed improbable to Lance, as most serial killers didn't willingly go twenty years between killings—assuming there hadn't been more victims with a different killer MO that kept the authorities from connecting the dots—it was something he could hardly rule out. Not when Bonnie's murder was still unsolved and languishing in the department's cold case files as essentially gone and forgotten.

Lance squared his broad shoulders and stood tall, at six feet two and a half inches of solid muscle, wearing the standard Hawaii-detective casual attire of a print polo shirt, khaki pants and dark boat shoes. He zeroed his deep blue eyes on the medical examiner, Dr. Ernest Espiritu, as he worked on the decedent.

Espiritu was slender, shorter and in his midfifties, with coarse short black-and-white hair worn in a faux hawk. He had brown rectangle eyeglasses and was wearing a lab coat, scrubs and latex gloves. "The decedent's death was due to strangulation," the ME said straightforwardly. "To be more specific, Ms. Hussey died as a result of cerebral hypoxia, which came from her blood vessels being compressed, cutting off oxygen to the brain. Judging by the ligature abrasions on her neck, I'd say that she was murdered by someone most likely using a leather belt as the lethal weapon of choice."

Lance cringed at the thought of someone dying so

cruelly, bringing him back to his sister and the un-
nerving similarities in the manner of death. "Were
there any signs of a sexual assault?" he asked curiously, knowing Bonnie had fortunately not suffered
in that regard as well.

Espiritu shook his head. "As far as I can determine,
this death did not involve sexual victimization of the
decedent. Of course, the assailant's true motives and
own interpretation of the attack will be up to you to
determine."

"I understand." Lance was less interested in trying to psychoanalyze the unsub, leaving that to others more qualified, than establishing if they were
a repeat offender. And, therefore, likely to commit
murder again. Or, as it concerned Lance, had already
perpetrated at least one murder. He left the medical
examiner's office on Iwilei Road in his department-
subsidized green Ford Explorer Timberline SUV for
the short drive back to the HPD. Running a hand
through his fudge-brown hair, worn in a buzz-cut
fade, Lance thought about his sister and her tragic
end. He was only seventeen at the time and had made
plans to visit her in Hawaii the following summer,
when Bonnie would show him the ropes in surf-
ing, parasailing and even scuba diving—all of which
she had mastered since living in Honolulu. But that
never happened, leaving him to learn on his own.
Their parents grieved her loss with him till the very

ends of their own lives, one from a heart attack, the other cancer.

Bonnie's unsolved death was the reason Lance had left St. Louis and joined the United States Marines, where he was stationed at the Marine Corps Base Hawaii in Kaneohe Bay, on the Mokapu Peninsula on the windward side of Oahu. He wanted to be close to her on some level, if only in spirit, on an island Bonnie loved. After completing his service, Lance joined the Honolulu Police Department and reached the rank of detective sergeant. Now at age thirty-seven, he specialized in homicide investigations, hoping to bring closure to families that his own family never had. Through the years he had learned as much as he could about Bonnie's murder, wanting to solve the crime and, if possible, bring her killer to justice. But much to Lance's chagrin, he had failed, as it remained a cold case and seemingly out of his reach to crack.

Lance blamed this vexation and, some would call it, obsession, for his failed personal relationships that never seemed to work, as though he were impeded by a ghost he couldn't shake. In particular, he couldn't help but think about the one woman who'd gotten away from him. Nearly three years ago, he found something special with Caroline Yashima, a gorgeous and sexier-than-she-knew investigator for the Hawaii Department of the Attorney General, Criminal Justice Division. If he'd had any sense, he would never have turned his back on her. Or what they had. Not a day had gone by since that he didn't regret walking away and not giving them a chance to see how things would play out. But he was too caught up in regrets, self-pity and timidity to find happiness with someone. He'd messed up and now he had to live with it. He imagined that by now Caroline had someone else in her life who could give her all the love she deserved and got as much in return. She certainly had a lot to offer any man worthy of her. Hell, maybe she even had a ring on her finger. One that should have been his. He doubted he'd ever get the chance at a do-over. But a guy could dream, couldn't he?

Lance came back down to earth as he arrived at the PD. Inside, he headed straight for the office of Lieutenant Dorian Powell, who led the Criminal Investigation Division, wanting to update him on the current homicide investigation. Beyond that, Lance planned to express his intentions to look into the possibility that Bonnie's killer and the unsub responsible for the death of Jill Hussey could well be one and the same, as unlikely as it may have seemed with the time gap. If the unsub were still alive, they could be anywhere by now on the islands, mainland or another place in the world. Since the lieutenant had been one of the detectives investigating Bonnie's murder, Lance knew that the fact that it remained an unsolved case had gnawed at him as well through the years. So why would he oppose reopening the investigation? Especially if they could potentially solve two homicide cases at once.

Powell was sitting at his cottage-style L-shaped desk, shuffling some papers, or pretending to, when Lance walked into the office. A large window provided a bird's-eye view of the larger office with the detectives' cubicles. It seemed as though Powell, who was African American, forty-five and solidly built with a shaved bald head and sharp black eyes, had been waiting for Lance as he offered him one of two padded stacking chairs.

"What have you got for me?" Powell asked equably, reclining in his high-backed cream-colored leather chair.

Lance briefed him on the medical examiner's findings and was just about to get into the similarities between this case and Bonnie's when the lieutenant seemed to be one step ahead of him.

"Between the manner of death and the missing shoe, it leads one to believe that we could be looking at the same killer, which would make the unsub a serial killer—or an intentional copycat killer—in your sister's murder and that of Jill Hussey. To that end, I've asked the Hawaii Department of the Attorney General, CJD to have one of their cold homicide investigators take a fresh look into Bonnie's death and see if any of the dots connect."

"Really?" Lance's thick brows shot up in surprise

that the lieutenant had asked for assistance from another law enforcement agency, though he was pleased that they were on the same page about reinvestigating his sister's murder. "Isn't that what we have our own Cold Case Unit for?" Not that he was opposed to working with the attorney general's CJD in reviving the investigation that had stalled over the years in the HPD and CCU and given way to other more recent cold cases. Quite the contrary—he had no problem with the joint operation, having done one before successfully. Lance couldn't help but think about Caroline Yashima, whom he'd first met when their paths crossed while investigating an environmental-related homicide. Too bad she wasn't working the cold cases for the CJD, as it could have been interesting to work with her again, if nothing else.

Powell looked a little uncomfortable as he continued, "Yeah, I think we need to step outside the box in this instance. Especially after the CJD solved the Harvey Nakao murder." Lance acknowledged as much and was impressed, though he had been too wrapped up in his own cases to follow it closely. "Anyhow, I've asked CJD administrator Vera Miyasato to assist and she's sending over a detective. Of course, you'll coordinate your current investigation with the attorney general's cold case investigator efforts and see if we can land one or two fish in solving these disturbing cases."

"Sounds like a plan," Lance readily agreed. "So, when do I meet this investigator?"

"How about right now?" Powell jutted his chin. "She's been waiting at your desk for, I'd say, the last ten minutes or so."

Lance grinned guiltily as he stood up. "In that case, guess I better not keep her waiting any longer."

"You better not," the CID lieutenant concurred. After a beat, he added pensively, "Hope we both get what we're looking for, Warner—"

"So do I." Lance left on that note and made his way through the detectives' maze, as he liked to refer to the work space they occupied when not in the field. As he neared his oak desk, he saw only the back of the dark-haired, small-boned woman sitting in a side chair. She seemed to sense his approach, for she turned around in that instant, giving Lance a start as he looked into the stunning face of the one woman, apart from his sister, he'd never been able to get out of his mind. Caroline Yashima. "Caroline…" he whispered, suddenly feeling at a loss for words.

The same apparently wasn't true for her, as Caroline uttered in a sharp voice that countered her delicate features, "Glad you finally showed up, Detective Sergeant Warner. Nice to see you again too."

Chapter Two

Lance was again tongue-tied as he took in his still-as-gorgeous-as-ever former girlfriend, who was probably the last person he expected to lay eyes on as the CJD cold case investigator he had been paired with to look into Bonnie's death. Something told him—perhaps the hard gaze of Caroline's cappuccino-brown eyes staring back at him—that this wasn't her choice. Not that he could blame her reluctance to be in his presence in any manner. He had pushed her away and was getting what he deserved with the cold shoulder. Was it too late to make things right between them? Or had that ship sailed?

"So, are we going to do this or what?" Caroline broke the stilted silence between them.

"Yes." Lance made himself speak up. There would be time for future reflection and finding a way to move forward later. He sat in his well-worn black leather desk chair and tried to keep it professional for now. "Sorry to keep you waiting. I just got back from the Department of the Medical Examiner to get the autopsy results on Jill Hussey. The ME confirmed that she was strangled last night." He choked on that note in thinking about Bonnie. "Beyond that, my boss, Lieutenant Dorian Powell, never mentioned the name of the CJD investigator coming over."

"Would it have mattered?" She batted her curly lashes daringly. "Don't answer that. Let's not go there. We both have a job to do and I just want to do my part in trying to solve your sister's murder, whether or not it's related to your current investigation."

"Fair enough." Was it truly that easy for her to sweep what they had under the rug? Or was this merely her putting up a wall so she wouldn't be hurt by him again? Either way, Lance had to respect that. He wasn't looking to intrude upon her life any more than necessary to conduct their joint and separate investigations. But if she were able to close the case on Bonnie's death, he would be forever grateful, even if it was in the course of Caroline's professional assignment.

He supposed it would be out-of-bounds and maybe a bit too clichéd to tell her she hadn't changed a bit. If she had, it was definitely for the better, Lance thought, as he again took in her brown-eyed beauty within a slim oval light-skinned face with a dainty nose and small mouth. Her straight dark hair was in a tight bun, but was clearly just as lengthy as he remembered, with eye-skimming bangs. Even seated, it was obvious to him that she hadn't put an ounce on her streamlined figure in the two and a half years since he'd last seen her. He blocked out pleasing thoughts of them being together in the carnal sense, knowing he needed to focus on what brought them to this point in time. "So, how long have you been investigating cold cases?" he asked curiously.

"Nearly seven months," Caroline stated, sitting back. "I got tired of investigating environmental crimes, fraud cases and the like. When this opportunity came along, I jumped on it."

Lance recalled that, like him, there was a cold case in her family. It was one reason he'd formed a bond with Caroline, even if he'd thrown it away. "So you were the one working the Harvey Nakao case?" he deduced.

She nodded. "It was challenging, to say the least," she confessed. "Forty years on ice is a long time. But with persistence and a few breaks, I was able to identify his killer and give Nakao's family closure."

This impressed Lance more than he cared to admit. It would impress him even more if she could achieve the same results in figuring out who killed Bonnie, because that would halve the length of time the crime was cold for compared to Nakao's. "Glad you were able to do that for Harvey Nakao's loved ones."

"I try my best." Caroline downplayed it. "It's all any of us can do, really."

"I agree." He gave her a tiny grin while wishing their reunion was under more favorable circumstances. "Sometimes, that's still not enough." At least that was the case in his experience. It didn't mean he ever quit the fight for what was right. Except maybe where it concerned the missteps in his love life.

"True." She paused and clasped her small hands. "Do you really think that Jill Hussey's murder is related to the death of your sister so many years ago?"

That's a good question, Lance thought, rubbing his jawline. And a hard one as well. Almost two decades was a long stretch for Bonnie's killer to have laid low, only to return to kill again as though no time had gone by. Was this even plausible? Lance's gut feelings told him that the connection was there in some way, shape or form. But gut feelings did not solve crimes. Especially those too close to home. Not without the right help from a like-minded person. "I think it's a good possibility," he told Caroline. "The fact that the unsub was deliberate in walking away from the scene of the crime with one of the victim's shoes in both instances, and nothing else, strikes me as more than a little suspicious. When you combine that with the strangulation deaths of both women with apparently a leather belt, it suggests a pattern of behavior that can't be ignored."

"I was thinking the same thing," she said. "At the very least, it appears that whoever murdered Jill Hussey was knowledgeable about your sister's death and either wanted to recreate it as a copycat or literally pick up where Bonnie's killer left off decades later, almost as if to taunt the authorities in letting us know the unsub is back."

Lance gritted his teeth at the notions, conceding that one possibility was just as likely as the other. It would take a sick mind to want to follow the footsteps of a killer. And equally fiendish to want to start up again and take away another innocent life. Whichever way this went, Lance braced himself for what was to come. Including the prospect that the two killings were unrelated and Bonnie's death could remain forever unsolved. He met Caroline's cerebral eyes and asked, "Have you talked to Detective Eliza Taracena of the Cold Case Unit yet?"

Caroline shook her head. "No, I came here first to touch base with you. It seemed like a good place to start the investigation."

"It was," Lance concurred, knowing this was what their respective bosses, Lieutenant Powell and Administrator Miyasato, wanted in seeing if the two cases were, in fact, related. In any event, he welcomed reopening the investigation into Bonnie's murder, as well as the opportunity to reconnect with Caroline in any way he could. She was the one who got away, Lance was willing to concede, for worse and not better. "Why don't we head over there now and see what she can tell us about the original investigation into Bonnie's death?"

"Sounds like a plan."

Caroline got to her feet and Lance saw that she was indeed every bit as appealing as before, even if his mind should have been elsewhere. He couldn't help but like what she presented as the complete package that likely had been given to another man by now in a relationship. The notion irked Lance for some reason, though he tried not to let it show. He rose, towering over her five-five stature, but he still considered their heights a good fit when they were together. "Before we pay the CCU a visit, I'll introduce you to the other detective involved with the investigation into Jill Hussey's death," Lance said, wanting to keep everyone on the same page for achieving the best results in the joint investigation.

"That would be great," Caroline said, and he sensed that this would go a long way in making her feel part of the team and facilitate cooperation between their departments moving forward.

Lance found the gray-eyed Detective Hugo Gushi-ken at his desk. At forty-eight, he looked older with a thick build and thinning gray hair swept backward. On his third marriage, having tied the knot for the second time to wife number one, he had five kids.

Though Lance was childless while pushing forty, he still dreamed of someday becoming a father and keeping the family going with no one else left to do so. He hoped the right woman was out there who wanted a family as well. He recalled that Caroline had felt that way when they were together. He didn't imagine that had changed. The absence of a ring on her finger told Lance she likely wasn't married. Maybe there was still hope that they could find their way back to one another. Or was the idea totally unrealistic, all things considered?

Gushiken shook hands with Caroline. "Heard that you solved the Harvey Nakao murder."

"I did," she told him proudly, "but had help in doing so."

"I know that Warner has never been able to rest easily while his sister's death remained an open and unsolved case. If we are talking about the same killer as Jill Hussey's, meaning the perp's still alive and as dangerous as ever, I'd like nothing better than to close the books on both cases at once."

"Wouldn't we all," Lance said in spite of some misgivings creeping in, as if the passage of time would somehow be a natural and maybe impenetrable barrier to bringing Bonnie's killer to justice. But what if that weren't the case?

"With any luck," Caroline said, glancing from one to the next, "taking another hard look at Bonnie's death and the investigation into it will yield positive results. If those can help solve your latest homicide, all the better."

"Yeah, I'm with you there." Gushiken made a face. "Last thing we need is a serial killer running amok on the island." He eyed Lance. "And if we are looking at two different killers, hopefully we can figure it out and, in the process, allow your sister the peace in the afterlife she deserves."

"I appreciate that." Lance was moved, knowing that Gushiken had been on the force when Bonnie was killed, though he was only a rookie cop and was not involved in the investigation. Now a hard-nosed homicide detective, Gushiken was just as dedicated as Lance was in solving crimes they investigated in the modern era. But Lance suddenly found himself with a new mission: pursuing an old crime equally fervently with the help of his ex-lover turned cold case investigator, Caroline. Fortunately, she seemed just as determined to find out who took the life of his sister that September day, twenty years ago.

CAROLINE SNUCK A peek at Lance as they walked into the Cold Case Unit of the Honolulu Police Department. Even if she was still angry with him for shutting the door on their relationship just when it seemed like the sky was the limit, she had to admit that he was every bit as handsome as the day he walked out on her thirty months ago, though it seemed like only yesterday. His square-shaped face and chiseled jaw-line went well with those enticing deep blue eyes and Roman nose. She even liked the buzz cut he wore these days, in place of the angular fringe haircut she remembered. And as for the rest of him, if anything, Lance was even more solid in his physical being, suggesting to her that he still kept in shape through the water sports he loved.

She pushed back the thoughts of a good-looking physical specimen who was great in and out of bed, till he moved out of her life, as Caroline realized it did her no good to reminisce about something that ultimately caused her pain. All she wanted from Lance in this instance was his cooperation as she investigated the death of his sister, with the expectation that its mystery could be unraveled and Lance could finally get past this and on with his life. *Even if that life no longer involves me*, Caroline told herself as they were approached by a petite and attractive woman in her early thirties with brunette hair in a pixie bob cut.

"I'm Detective Eliza Taracena," she said, planting small hazel eyes on Caroline. "You must be the cold case investigator from the attorney general's CJD?"

"Caroline Yashima," she acknowledged and shook her hand.

"Lieutenant Powell briefed me that you were coming and why. Nice to meet you."

"You too."

Eliza faced Lance. "Detective Warner," she said in a serious tone.

"Eliza," he responded equably. He told Caroline, "We touched base recently on another case I worked on."

"I see." Caroline gave a little smile, feeling relieved somewhat that their association seemed lim-

ited and strictly professional. This went entirely
against the grain of her intent to stay in the professional lane herself with her former boyfriend.

Eliza regarded the detective. "I know how difficult
this must be for you in reopening the investigation into
your sister's death. I'll do whatever I can to assist."

Lance nodded favorably and said, "Mahalo."

"Why don't we head over to my desk," Eliza told
them, and led the way. Over her shoulder, she said,
"I've pulled up everything we have on computer and
can send it to you both. The rest will be in the evidence room."

"Anything stand out to you in your perusal of the
information?" Caroline asked curiously as she stood
on one side of the cluttered desk and Lance the other.

"Not really." Eliza spoke apologetically as she
sat before her laptop. "From what I can see, on the
night in question, Bonnie Warner was accosted by
an unknown assailant inside her own apartment—
and strangled." Her voice cracked and Caroline knew
it was out of respect for Lance, who stood there si-
lently and didn't even blink with despair, as though
he had stilled himself from the pain. "Oddly, the perp
took off with one of Bonnie's shoes and apparently
nothing else, while leaving no discernible DNA or
fingerprints that we could match with any others in
the system. With the advances made in DNA analysis and other evidentiary processes since the origi-

nal investigation, we might have better results this time around."

"That's what I'm banking on," Lance said bluntly.

"Along with any additional findings that might point the finger at the killer," Caroline added, knowing that biological evidence that was weakened due to age or degradation or compromised in other ways would still make the case challenging to crack, even with modern scientific developments.

"Whatever it takes," he concurred, gazing at her.

"Of course," Eliza agreed as well. "We have the names of the original suspects and witnesses to go through and hopefully track down, if necessary, in trying to identify the unsub."

Lance nodded. "If any of them can be cross-checked with anyone we find is involved in the current homicide-by-strangulation investigation, all the better."

Caroline tried to imagine a killer so brazen to have lain dormant for two decades only to strike again, while seemingly wanting to play a renewed game of cat and mouse by recreating the original murder. Was this for real? Or a very clever copycat killer? If so, Caroline wondered if she had enough to work with to identify Bonnie's murderer.

Her reverie was broken when Eliza uttered, "Why don't we head over to the evidence room and you can have a look at what's there that may or may not provide solid clues to work with in the investigation…"

"Good idea," Lance quickly agreed, and Caroline found herself eager to see the stored cold case evidence, or lack thereof, in the murder of Lance's older sister.

The evidence room was located in a secured-access vault. Caroline and Lance were handed a pair of latex gloves and led to a storage row with compact mobile shelving containing case evidence in bins, boxes and envelopes. Eliza used a warehouse ladder to retrieve a large cardboard box off a top shelf and placed it on a metal table. It had a barcode number that corresponded with the unsolved death of Bonnie Warner.

"Here you are," Eliza said. "Every piece of evidence has been logged, including dates and times and who collected what. Obviously, it fell short of having what was needed to make an arrest and successfully prosecute someone. But things change..."

As they opened the box, Caroline spotted the single bagged high-heeled thong sandal. It looked brand-new, with the other sandal missing and possibly still in the possession of the person who took it and her life. Caroline felt a chill at the thought of going through items that either belonged to Lance's sister or were sad reminders of Bonnie's ordeal, leading to her death. These included crime scene photographs; physical and circumstantial evidence that was typically paired with witness identification; witness and victim statements; and fingerprints and DNA. In most cases involving crimes of violence, such evidence was often enough to put the perps away. But not in cold crimes, where justice was either delayed or outright denied. Caroline hoped the latter wouldn't hold true when taking another shot at it.

I can only imagine how difficult this moment must be for Lance, Caroline told herself as she lifted her eyes to his. She had seen the anguish in them before, during their time together. Even when he did his best to seem as if it was all behind him, she'd sensed it was always there in some way, shape or form, and he was unable to break away from it entirely. Would solving the case be the closure he needed? Or would he never be able to let go?

"Bonnie deserved a hell of a lot better than having her entire life come down to a few boxed items," Lance grumbled, lifting the bag with the thong sandal, before dropping it back inside the box.

"She'll get something better in the end," Caroline promised while resisting the urge to reach out and touch him. Having second thoughts about assuring him that this would come out satisfactory, she said, "If there's any chance at all of bringing this case to closure, working together should help achieve this goal."

"Thanks." He nodded warmly. "Means a lot coming from you."

She took that as a compliment, in spite of their history, nodding back. "I meant every word." How could she not? No reason why either of them should let past regrets prevent them from professional cooperation. "We'll need to have all the clothing and other such evidence retested for any DNA that might have been unattainable before."

"Yeah," Lance agreed while pouring through more of the contents. "Maybe some prints can be pulled as well and those will lead somewhere."

That too sounded plausible to Caroline, knowing the advances made on that front over the years. At the very least, they might be able to match the forensic evidence from one case to the other and identify a possible suspect.

"By the way, the lead detective in the original investigation was Detective Roger Nielsen," Eliza informed them. "He retired three years later after being shot in the line of duty. Did some digging and found out that he still lives in Honolulu. I can give you his address."

"That sounds great," Caroline said. Picking the brain of the first detective to take on this case was a logical step toward reinvestigating it, and she was certain Lance would agree. Maybe Detective Nielsen could provide some insight that could be useful in their current probe. "Who else worked the case?" she asked curiously.

"Actually, Lieutenant Powell was one of the initial investigators, back when he was a detective," Eliza responded. "Given his current rank, he would certainly be in a good position to recognize the similarities in an old and new case."

"Seems so," Lance remarked thoughtfully. "Since I've known him, the lieutenant has expressed regret that Bonnie's death was never solved. The fact that another woman has been murdered in a like manner only brought that to the forefront for him and me."

And now me too, Caroline mused. If Bonnie's murder weighed on Lieutenant Powell through the years, she imagined the same was true for Detective Nielsen. As far as she was concerned, it was never too late to make things right for them and Lance.

Chapter Three

Lance drove as he and Caroline headed to Roger Nielsen's house. He had never met the retired detective before, but had heard Lieutenant Powell speak about him from time to time as someone who had a good track record solving cases. With the exception of Bonnie's murder, which had stumped the detective. Now, nearly two decades later, the unsub may have come back to once again cause pain to those left behind as a result of the killings. If this was the case, Lance hoped Nielsen could help him and Caroline nail the perp. He was sure the lieutenant felt the same in encouraging them to see if they could connect any dots between past and present.

Turning to Caroline, who seemed caught up in her own thoughts, Lance wondered if any of those thoughts pertained to their previous relationship and how things ended. Was it weird for her to have him back in her life, in a manner of speaking? Or was he projecting how strange it felt for him? But it was a good weird, if that was possible. The truth was he had dreamed of one day reuniting with her, even if only in friendship. Was this the closest he would ever get to that? If so, he wouldn't look a gift horse in the mouth. Even if the circumstances that brought them together were uncomfortable, to say the least, and had yet to play themselves out.

With silence inside the car unsustainable, Lance said the first thing that came to mind, awkward as it may have sounded. "So, how have you been?"

Caroline took a breath and answered succinctly without looking at him. "Busy."

Haven't we all, he thought, but found himself unable or unwilling to leave it at that. "I mean beyond work."

She faced him with a stiff lower lip. "If you're asking if I've been moping around feeling sorry for myself since the day you abruptly ended things between us, the answer is no."

"Guess I deserved that." Lance focused on the road. He hadn't felt it would be easy trying to get back into a door that he had foolishly shut. Didn't mean he intended to give up. Or push her too far, too soon. "I wasn't trying to get the scoop on your love life or anything," he told her. Maybe he was on some level, but some things might be best not knowing. He glanced at her again. "I just wondered if you were okay in your life at this time. If this is overstepping, my apologies."

"I'm fine." Her features softened. "Enjoying life

when I can. Not taking things too seriously, apart from when on the job."

Lance never knew Caroline to be too serious, which was one of the things that attracted him to her. She could have fun with the best of them, but knew when to shut it down. He wanted to delve deeper into what constituted enjoyment of life for her, such as her love life, but decided this wasn't the time. "Good to know," he told her.

"And how about you? Are you still scuba diving and otherwise playing in the water?"

He grinned. "Yeah, it's still my thing, when I find the time." Being in the water had been more fun, Lance realized, when he was able to do so with Caroline, who had gotten out of her comfort zone in a willingness to meet him halfway, if not more. He missed those days, even though they had gone away by his own choice.

"Why am I not surprised?" There was an amusement to her voice that caused a stir in him.

"I'm an open book," Lance said wryly. *Except when I choose to close it*, he thought.

"If you say so."

Before he could comment further, they had reached their destination, a single-family home near downtown Honolulu on Kokea Street. There was a red Volkswagen Taos SUV parked in the driveway. Lance sighed. "Let's see what Nielsen has to say about the case he left hanging for us to try to figure out." Not that he wanted to point any fingers, but Lance had always wondered if the original detectives, including his boss, had done enough to catch Bonnie's killer. What key clues had they missed? Or was he merely unreasonably looking to blame someone other than the perp responsible for her death?

"Yes, let's do this," Caroline concurred, seeming eager to evade talking about Lance, or them, for that matter. He admitted that this was probably for the best, seeing that she had already moved on in life without him.

They left the car and bypassed a cluster of golden cane palms before ringing the doorbell. When the door opened, a thin woman in her midfifties with platinum hair in a spunky pixie style and dimpled cheeks said, "Aloha. Can I help you?"

"Is Roger Nielsen home?" Lance asked.

"Yes, he is. I'm his wife, Dorothy. What's this all about?"

Before he could answer, Lance heard from behind her a bass voice ask casually, "Did I hear someone mention my name?" A man in his late fifties of medium build, with gray hair in a balding fade cut, a deep tan and blue-gray eyes with bags underneath, appeared. "I'm Roger Nielsen." He was wearing a short-sleeved blue shirt that had white plumeria flowers on it, stone-colored cargo shorts and slide sandals. He was also using a wooden walking cane.

Lance resisted flashing his identification. "I'm Detective Lance Warner of the Honolulu PD and this is Caroline Yashima, a cold case investigator for the Hawaii Department of the Attorney General, Criminal Justice Division. We've reopened the investigation into the murder of Bonnie Warner, my sister," he added, seeing no reason to hide his special interest in the case.

"Ah, yes," Nielsen said. "Dorian Powell told me you might be dropping by. Nice to meet you both." He stuck out a thick hand and Lance shook first, followed by Caroline. "Come in…"

They followed him inside the spacious one-story home. A quick scan and Lance saw contemporary furnishings atop hardwood flooring. He turned back to Nielsen, who stated contritely, "I'm sorry about what happened to your sister. The investigation was a long time ago, but I still remember it like it was yesterday. Like Powell, I'm glad you're giving it a second look and happy to do whatever I can to help."

"Mahalo," Caroline said in an appreciative tone of voice.

Lance also welcomed anything he could provide that might yield useful information, even if for the most part he believed they would need to essentially start from scratch in putting the pieces together to bridge the corridors of time.

"Have a seat," Nielsen directed, and proffered his long arm toward a pair of white fabric accent chairs in the living room. After they sat, he asked, "Can we get you something to drink? I know you're on duty, so alcohol's out. But we have bottled water, coffee, tea and lemonade."

"Lemonade sounds good," Caroline said, smiling.

Lance followed suit, wanting to keep this visit as cozy as possible, suspecting she felt the same.

Nielsen regarded his wife. "Honey, can you get them some lemonade?"

Dorothy nodded. "Sure. You want anything?"

"I'll have a beer."

"Coming right up."

As she headed for the kitchen, Nielsen sat on a maroon sofa, leaning the cane against it. He winced. "Left the force much sooner than I'd planned, courtesy of a bullet that landed all too close to my spine after I served a warrant on a suspect in a drive-by shooting. The doctor told me if the bullet had landed an inch over, I'd either be dead or paralyzed today. Thank goodness for small favors, right? The shooter wasn't so lucky. Took him out before he could finish the job. Anyway, you're not here to talk about me." He took a breath. "Bonnie Warner's death hit everyone in the department pretty hard, on account of the fact that she had come to Honolulu to go to college and someone decided to end her dream prematurely."

His wife came back with the lemonade on a tray and handed a glass to Caroline and then Lance before setting the tray on an oval walnut coffee table.

Dorothy sat beside her husband and gave him a beer bottle, while having nothing to drink herself.

"I looked at the file on the investigation, Detective Nielsen," Caroline said respectfully. "Was there anything about the crime scene itself that caught your attention? And what are your thoughts on the unsub taking one of the victim's shoes, I assume as a trophy…?"

Nielsen thought about the questions while sipping his beer. "On the first question, yeah, I found it odd that there was really nothing out of place in Ms. Warner's apartment. Apart from the body. For most such indoor homicides, there is an indication of the violence through disarray and such in the process. But for this one, it appears as though the victim put up little to no struggle. Maybe Ms. Warner was caught so off guard that she didn't have time to react. Or the perp was somehow able to get the job done in short order and leave everything virtually intact, before vacating the premises posthaste." He sucked in a breath and tasted more beer. "As to the missing shoe, not sure what to make of it. Apart from being, as you say, a trophy to have as a keepsake of the crime, the unsub may have had a foot or shoe fetish. We were never really able to figure that out."

To Lance, that wasn't good enough. He needed more from the lead investigator on his sister's death and killer, especially in light of the most recent homicide that drew parallels. "What about the suspects?"

He threw the question at him. "Did any of them seem solid enough to warrant a second look? Or even a third, for that matter?"

Nielsen shifted uncomfortably. "Yeah, we interviewed everyone who didn't have a solid alibi multiple times, but nothing stuck in terms of being able to make an arrest. It certainly wasn't from lack of trying."

"Maybe you should have tried harder," Lance snapped, knowing right away he had overstepped after getting a look of disapproval from Caroline.

Nielsen's jaw tightened. "Listen, Warner, I understand that you're still hurting that your sister was murdered twenty years ago, but don't come into my house and accuse me of not doing my job. As a homicide detective yourself, you know that not all cases are solved. At least not in short order. I spent three years trying to find your sister's killer—even when I wasn't on official duty—till I was forced into early retirement by a bullet. The relentless pursuit cost me my first marriage." He sighed and grabbed the hand of his current wife. "Fortunately, I found Dorothy here and got a second chance at happiness. I won't let you put a damper on that."

"Love you too, honey," she murmured affectionately, squeezing his hand.

"Sorry, that was never my intention," Lance said guiltily, realizing this was shifting in the wrong direction. The blame game never did much good where it concerned homicide investigations. "I know you did your job to the best of your ability, along with others investigating Bonnie's murder. We only came to see you because of a new development. Last night, a young woman was found strangled in her apartment. One of her shoes was missing. Just like with Bonnie. We believe the two cases may be connected."

Caroline added politely, after sipping lemonade, "We were hoping that, with your knowledge of the original case, you might offer some insight as to whether we could be looking at the same killer."

Nielsen's jaw relaxed. "I seriously doubt that it's the same perpetrator," he said flatly. "Two decades is a long time between such killings for the killer to just up and decide to strike again." He put the beer bottle to his mouth. "Not sure about the copycat angle either. Could be coincidental, unless the new killer happens to be a history buff. Even then, I don't think the murder of Bonnie Warner remained a hot news story locally for very long, as other crimes took center stage, for better or worse."

Though Lance fumed at the thought that Bonnie's death was essentially pushed aside when the next murder arose, he knew that this was the nature of the beast when it concerned criminality. There was always a new crime to focus on, often at the expense of old ones. But now that the opportunity had presented itself to go after Bonnie's killer, Lance vowed not to let it slip away. Someone would be held accountable.

By the time they left the house, he felt they were on reasonably good terms with Nielsen, in case further communication was needed. Indeed, after the retired detective walked them to the door, he put a large hand on Lance's shoulder, looked him in the eye and said in earnest, "Keep me posted." Lance fully intended to do just that.

"SORRY YOU HAD to go through that," Caroline said during the drive back to the HPD. She understood how difficult it had to be for Lance to have a face-to-face with the ex-detective who led the investigation into the death of Lance's sister. At the same time, antagonizing someone who had obviously tried but failed to catch the killer was probably not the best move. to his credit, Lance was able to smartly pivot away from the attitude and back toward a more conciliatory working relationship with Roger Nielsen.

"It's par for the course," Lance remarked from behind the wheel. "Losing my big sister the way I did and still searching for answers as to why can make you a little crazy sometimes."

"You think?" She spoke lightheartedly, knowing he was anything but crazy as a loving little brother, dedicated cop and former lover.

"I shouldn't have treated Nielsen like the enemy, though. My bad."

While not arguing the point, Caroline said, "You

smoothed things over. Now we move on to trying to unravel the mystery, if at all possible."

"Agreed." Lance glanced at her. "I'm glad we get to do this together, no matter how it turns out."

She felt the heat from his eyes. Or was it simply the nearness of their bodies that had her temperature rising a notch or two? "I feel the same," she responded honestly, even if the guarded part of her wanted to stay as far away from the man as possible.

After Lance dropped her off at her car and agreed to meet the following day to continue coordinating their efforts, Caroline headed back to her office. There, she made arrangements with the Scientific Investigation Section of the Honolulu PD to conduct new forensic tests on physical evidence collected in the Bonnie Warner cold case, including blood, fingerprints and fibers, to determine if there was anything different from the original results. She also wanted to see how the findings might stack up to analysis of DNA and the other crime scene data gathered by forensics in the murder of Jill Hussey.

Caroline drove on Punchbowl Street toward home, her thoughts occupied with the unexpected reunion with Lance, along with the investigation into his sister's death. She couldn't have imagined either beginning her day and had mixed feelings. Yes, she wanted to help Lance get some answers as to Bonnie's murder. But seeing the man again whom she had fallen hard for, only to have this shoved back in her face, still troubled Caroline. She had expected better of him. And now? Did she really want to go back there, open herself up to more pain, with no real upside other than to massage her wounded ego?

I'll try my best to resist the pull Lance still has on me, Caroline told herself, even when part of her relished the notion of them starting up again as a couple, if only in her overactive but unrealistic imagination. She arrived at her condominium on Ala Moana Boulevard and parked the car in her covered stall. Using her passkey, Caroline took the elevator up to the twentieth floor and her unit. Stepping inside, she took in the spacious two-bedroom, two-bathroom condo in Waikiki, a neighborhood of Honolulu on the south shore of Oahu. It had a gourmet kitchen with veined-marble countertops, floor-to-ceiling windows in the living room with amazing views, distressed-wood flooring and tropical-leaf-blade ceiling fans throughout. She had outfitted the condo with creamy white furniture and rustic wall accents.

Having purchased it a year after the breakup with Lance, Caroline was happy living there alone for the most part. But then there was that other part. A longing for companionship. His companionship. They had once talked about getting a place together, but it never got that far. She couldn't help but wonder what might have been had Lance not gotten cold feet in their relationship. *Guess I'll never know*, she told herself and headed into the kitchen.

After taking a bottle of red wine out of the re-
frigerator, Caroline poured herself half a glass and
brought it with her as she stepped out onto the lanai
and was immediately hit by the warm trade winds.
She had a nice view of Fort Derussy Beach Park,
along with Diamond Head—a volcanic tuff cone and
Hawaii's most familiar landmark—and the Pacific
Ocean. Even after spending her entire life there, save
for visits to the mainland and her ancestral home of
Japan, she never tired of this. *But it would still be
better if I had someone to share it with*, Caroline
thought, tasting the wine. Maybe it could still happen. Until such time, she wouldn't let it weigh her
down with what-ifs or what-never-happeneds.

Back inside, she decided before dinner to head
down to the recreation room on the premises to un-
wind after an eventful day. She pulled her hair loose
and then tied it in a high ponytail and changed into
a blue sports bra, gray workout shorts and white
running sneakers. Before she knew it, Caroline was
on a treadmill, speed walking alongside her friend
Rachelle Compagno. They had met at the condo and
quickly bonded as single and successful women who
liked to stay in shape and still wanted more in their
lives to make them complete.

Rachelle was a real estate attorney, a year older
than Caroline and trim and spirited, with green
eyes and mounds of crimson hair worn in a razored
and wavy shag when not braided while exercising.

She wore a matching mauve top and leggings with her running shoes. In the midst of hearing about Rachelle's latest dating app misadventures, Caroline couldn't resist mentioning her own unexpected relationship trip down memory lane. If only for the feedback.

Lifting an ultrathin brow, Rachelle asked without breaking her brisk walk, "You mean Lance, as in the detective who dumped you way back when?"

"The same," Caroline admitted, coloring as if embarrassed in so confirming. "But it's not what you think." She defended him, as much as herself. "I was assigned a cold case that happened to be the murder of Lance's sister twenty years ago. He's working a more recent homicide case that happens to have a similar MO."

"The woman who was strangled to death in Ewa Beach?" Caroline confirmed this. "Terrible way to die," Rachelle uttered.

"Yes, it was." Caroline recoiled at the mere thought. "Anyway, Lance and I are working together to see if we are talking about the same killer, which if true, could finally solve his sister's death."

"Hmm…" Rachelle grabbed her water bottle and took a drink. "That is too weird."

"Right?" Caroline agreed, wiping sweat from her brow with a towel. "But life can be that way sometimes."

"Maybe the universe is trying to tell you something," she suggested.

Caroline rolled her eyes, but was curious nonetheless. "Like what, hide somewhere among the stars to protect my heart?" She couldn't help but laugh at her own over-the-top words.

Rachelle chuckled. "Actually, just the opposite. Given that things between you were left hanging, if I read you correctly, this might either be a time to get real closure or leave the door wide open for whatever is meant to be—even if only to solve a cold case to both your benefit."

"You could be right," Caroline said thoughtfully while feeling the strain in her leg muscles. Reconnecting with Lance may well have been fate intervening on her behalf. Closure was a good thing, right? Or could she ever expect to be able to get the man out of her system when his presence had been so indelible, in spite of their breakup? "Or not," she blurted out unintentionally. "I think that, for now, I'll not overthink this and concentrate on digging deep into the cold case for some answers on Bonnie Warner's death."

Rachelle didn't object—like a legal argument—showing her support for whichever way things went in Caroline's reinvolvement with Lance. Caroline left it at that while slowing down on the treadmill and changing the topic of conversation.

By the time she got back to her condo, Caroline

was exhausted. She took a long shower, after which she made herself a salad, ate and called it an early night. Yet she found the sleep restless, as Lance, Bonnie and her faceless killer merged into something akin to a nightmare that begged to be snapped out of. But only if the case could have a worthwhile resolution for Caroline, Lance and, most of all, the sister he lost almost twenty years ago.

Chapter Four

Lance doubted he slept a wink as he got dressed for work the day after seeing Caroline again. The fact that she looked better than ever didn't help matters any as he tried to stay on point regarding the nature of their reunion. Finding out who killed Bonnie had to be front and center now that the possibility of an answer had been put on the table as the result of Jill Hussey's similar murder two days ago. Yet even with that reality staring him in the face like a dark cloud, there was no getting past the truth that he enjoyed spending time with the gorgeous cold case investigator. How could he not? He had never gotten her out of his system and no amount of denial would ever change that.

As Lance sipped on coffee and gobbled down cereal at the circular glass pedestal table in his open-concept dining area that flowed one way into the old-world-style kitchen and another right into the living room, he couldn't help but recall that it was in this very house he owned that he and Caroline had first made love. Sadly, it was also where they'd made love for the last time, causing him to have second thoughts about ending things between them impulsively. What had he been thinking? Or hadn't he bothered to think things through more clearly? If so, would he have done things differently?

Lance got out of his upholstered dining chair with the coffee mug in hand and walked across the stone-look tile flooring, glancing at the combination modern-and-retro living room furnishings, with bronze ceiling fans overhead. Eight years ago, he had purchased the single-story, three-bedroom marina-front home on Opihikao Place in Hawaii Kai, a mostly residential community in Honolulu County. It had always been his dream to own something with easy access to the water, and this was it. He stood at the sliding glass doors leading out to the covered lanai and, while sipping coffee, gazed out at the Koko Marina, where he had his own private dock—though an actual boat was still on his wish list. Beyond that were incredible views of Koko Crater and the Koolau Range. Caroline had loved the vantage point, especially when the sun was setting. And he had loved sharing his space with her when things were good between them. Had that ship really sailed for good? Or had their unlikely pairing offered a glimmer of hope for a reconciliation?

He finished off the coffee, brushed his teeth and

headed to work. His first order of business was to question Kurt Preston, the boyfriend of Jill Hussey. Preston had been picked up at a house construction site, where he was employed as a flooring installer. According to his rap sheet, he had once been arrested for assaulting another girlfriend, but she had refused to press charges. Had he gone one step further this time in attacking Hussey so she couldn't let him off the hook?

At the police station, Lance conferred briefly with Hugo Gushiken before stepping into the interrogation room where the suspect sat stone-faced at the metal table. He was on the lean side and blue-eyed with textured long and wavy hair. He was twenty-six years old, which told Lance that he would have been only six two decades ago. Meaning he couldn't have been Bonnie's killer. But he still could have been Jill Hussey's murderer.

Lance went on that notion as he sat across from Preston and said coolly, "Thanks for coming in." As if he had much of a choice in what wasn't a request. "I just need to ask you some questions about your late girlfriend, Jill Hussey."

Preston remained calm. "Look, I'm sorry that Jill is dead. I'll tell you whatever I can about my ex, though I'm not sure it would be of much help."

Lance homed in on the "ex" part. Was that going to be his defense—that they were no longer together when she died? "According to her roommate, Aimee

Browning, you two were still very much a couple. Are you saying she's lying?"

"I'm saying she's mistaken," he insisted, looking Lance straight in the eyes. "Jill and I have had an on-again, off-again relationship for the last year. It's been off for at least two weeks, after she caught me in bed with a friend named Sarah Mankiewicz. Jill was royally pissed and kicked me out of her apartment and that was that. Why she never told Aimee I can't say, other than maybe she was hoping we would one day get back together."

Lance thought the man seemed too sure of himself. At the same time, his story was plausible, as most young couples—and older ones too—had their ups and downs, some of which led to breakups. Maybe Jill was too ashamed to admit it to her roomie. "When did you last see Jill?" he asked him.

"About a week ago," Preston claimed.

"Where were you between eight and ten two nights ago?"

"At Sarah's place. With things over between me and Jill, I kind of moved on and in with Sarah, to see how things go."

A real stand-up guy, Lance mused, though conceded that his own track record when it came to relationships and doing the right thing was less than ideal. "I assume Ms. Mankiewicz can verify this?"

"Yeah, she can, since we spent the whole night together."

Lance knew this would be easy enough to verify. "Do you know anyone who would want to kill Jill?"

"No one I can think of." Preston scratched the side of his long nose. "Jill and I had our issues, but she didn't deserve to die like that. I have no idea who would kill her—or why—but it wasn't me."

Lance imagined that Jill could have started seeing someone else, to which her roommate wasn't the wiser, who could have strangled Hussey. Maybe someone she met on a flight. Or she'd been accosted by a total stranger. But given there was no sign of a break-in, it seemed more likely than not that she had invited her killer—male or female—inside her apartment. Even with that scenario, Lance still didn't see how this connected with the murder of his sister. Why the similar pattern? Could it all be coincidental from one killer to another? There were only so many ways to kill and collect items as trophies.

Lance gave the suspect a curious look. "Have you ever heard the name Bonnie Warner?"

"No." Preston did not flinch. "Should I?"

"She was my sister," Lance said straightforwardly. "Someone strangled her twenty years ago in Honolulu, much like the ligature strangulation of Jill Hussey. The killer was never caught."

"Sorry to hear that, man." He spoke with sincerity, giving no hint of consideration that the two killings could be perpetrated by the same unsub. "Maybe it's not too late for that to happen."

My thoughts precisely, Lance told himself. "I'll need the contact information for Sarah Mankiewicz to check out your alibi." After getting it, he stood and told Kurt Preston, "You're free to go for now. Someone will be in shortly to escort you out."

Lance stepped into the small room with a one-way window that looked into the interrogation room where Preston sat. "What do you think?" he asked Gushiken.

"Seems credible enough till proven to be the opposite," the detective said.

Lance nodded. "Yeah, check out his story. Assuming it holds up, we need to see if anyone else was in Jill Hussey's life, if she had issues with someone at work and even the type of relationship she had with the roommate and if she had any enemies." He took a breath. "If there are any red flags, we can go from there in investigating any possible connections with Bonnie's murder."

"I'm on it." Gushiken ran a hand across his mouth. "If there's something solid that links the cases, we'll find out whether we're dealing with a single killer or two killers playing the same flute."

Both possibilities unnerved Lance, but not nearly as much as the fear of one cold case becoming two cold cases, with the killer or killers never to be found and brought to justice.

CAROLINE WAS ADMITTEDLY a bit nervous for some reason as she sat in the office of Lieutenant Dorian

Powell, Lance's boss and the man who had asked Vera to have her look into Bonnie Warner's murder. Yes, there were questions Caroline had for him as one of the original investigators in Bonnie's death. But mainly, she felt pressure in taking on the case and not wanting to let anyone down in the search for answers, including the man before her. He sat at his desk while waiting for her to speak. She had decided to go it alone in the meeting this morning, knowing Lance was interrogating the boyfriend of Jill Hussey. That, after all, had to be Lance's top priority in a present-day homicide investigation. Whereas her own focus, first and foremost, was investigating a cold case murder that could be independent of the Jill Hussey murder, till proven otherwise. On top of that, Caroline didn't want it to be weird between Lance and the lieutenant, given the failure of the police department in solving Bonnie's murder when it had first occurred.

After taking a breath, Caroline said evenly, "So, we spoke with Detective Roger Nielsen yesterday about the Bonnie Warner case."

"That's good," Powell said, leaning forward across his desk. "Did he give you anything helpful?"

Nothing earth-shattering, she told herself. But she answered, "Detective Nielsen was cooperative in telling us what he recalled."

"I see." Powell sat back musingly. "The memory can sometimes fail us all over time. Hopefully,

Nielsen has still made himself available for any further inquiries?"

"He has," Caroline replied, wondering if they would need to talk to him again from this point on.

"How can I be of assistance?" the lieutenant asked.

Since you asked, she thought wryly. "As you were one of the detectives looking into Bonnie's murder, I was wondering if you could shed any further light on the investigation."

"I'll try." Powell took a breath. "By the time I arrived at the scene of the crime, Nielsen, as the lead detective, was already there and setting things in motion. Ms. Warner, Bonnie, was lying there, looking as though she were asleep on the floor. Obviously, she was never going to wake up. Someone had seen to that. With the scene secured, we went through the standard investigation, following leads wherever they took us." His face darkened. "Unfortunately, in spite of some promising leads along the way, we hit a dead end. It happens sometimes."

"Of course," Caroline conceded, aware that though just over half of the homicide cases in the country were cleared or solved every year, that still left a high percentage that were not. Many of those turned into cold and colder cases. That was when investigators like her came in. The lieutenant saw an opportunity to reopen the Bonnie Warner case and took it. But why not rely on the Cold Case Unit in his own department to investigate, instead of the Department of the Attorney General's Criminal Justice Division? "What are your thoughts on the murder of Jill Hussey in relation to Bonnie's murder?" Caroline asked interestedly.

Powell frowned. "Well, the similarities between the two are disturbing to me," he said point-blank. "Jill Hussey's death by ligature strangulation and her missing shoe brought back not-so-buried memories of the tragic death of Bonnie Warner that we were unable to get a handle on. Given that her brother is now one of my best detectives, it seemed more than worthwhile to give the homicide another look." He peered at her. "In case you're wondering, why go to your department to take the lead over my own very capable Cold Case Unit, I wanted to make sure there was no conflict of interest in the investigation, per se, between our cold case investigators and current homicide detectives in taking this on. The fact that the CJD—with you leading the way, I understand—was able to close the Harvey Nakao murder case impressed me. I'm hoping for similar results in the Bonnie Warner cold case, which would be a good thing as well for Detective Warner in having his sister's murder solved."

Caroline was moved by the lieutenant's delicate position, along with Lance's dual role in two investigations. The onus was on her to give them both some degree of closure, if at all possible. "I'll try not to let you down, sir," she told him sincerely.

"I'm counting on that." Powell nodded with a soft smile. "My door is always open if you need anything along the way."

She smiled back gratefully. "Thank you."

After leaving the office, Caroline hoped to find Lance and invite him to accompany her to the next stop in the investigation. But she was told that he had left the building to check out an alibi. *Oh, well*, Caroline thought, masking her disappointment, even as she knew that spending too much time with her ex was probably not in her best interests on the whole. She would go it alone this time in pursuit of information.

Back in her car, Caroline headed to talk with Shelley Pacheco, Bonnie's best friend at the time of her death when they were graduate students at UH Mānoa. Dr. Pacheco was now a professor at the school in the College of Tropical Agriculture and Human Resources.

Upon entering the small office, Caroline was greeted by the forty-five-year-old CTAHR professor, who was petite with short brunette hair in choppy layers. She wore round half-rim eyeglasses over brown eyes. "Aloha," she said, and offered her delicate hand.

Caroline shook it. "Nice to meet you, Dr. Pacheco."

"Please, call me Shelley," she said.

"All right." Caroline smiled and then, at Shelley's request, sat beside her in a wood-backed guest chair.

Shelley pushed her glasses back up her small nose.

"I must admit that you took me by surprise, Detective, when you said you were calling regarding Bonnie Warner. It's been so long since—"

"I understand how difficult it must be to have to go back there," Caroline told her sympathetically. "But, as I mentioned, we have reopened the investigation into Bonnie's death, hoping to find answers that weren't there before. As her best friend, I was hoping you might remember something, anything, that could help identify her killer."

Shelley twisted her lips musingly. "Well, as I told the police back then, there was that creepy janitor who worked in her apartment building. He seemed to be leering at us every time we saw him. Bonnie was a little freaked by it, but wasn't really in a good position to move. Other than that, nothing comes to mind as to who could've killed her."

"George Tacang, the janitor, was investigated and nothing came out of it," Caroline noted. "What about Bonnie's ex-boyfriend, Bradley Nolte? I understand that they broke up six months before she was murdered. Could he have wanted to harm her, maybe as retaliation for ending the relationship?"

"I don't think so," Shelley offered quickly. "Bradley was a jerk for cheating on Bonnie, but not a murderer. He didn't exactly try to win her back. Like many college guys, he simply moved on to other conquests without apparently giving it a second thought."

Or maybe he had, Caroline told herself. It wouldn't

have been the first time that an unfaithful person tried to worm their way back into the relationship and, when that failed, simply snapped. But Nolte's alibi of being with his latest conquest had held up. Unless she had lied for him. Or vice versa, and she'd been willing to kill to hang on to him.

"I don't suppose you kept in touch with Bradley over the years?" Caroline hadn't had the chance to search for him as yet. Maybe he still lived on Oahu.

"I haven't," she said, "not after what he put Bonnie through. But I couldn't help but keep tabs on him. After graduation, Bradley became a big shot hedge fund manager in Honolulu." Her tone dropped. "Unfortunately, he died in a car accident about ten years ago. Left behind a wife and four children."

"Sorry to hear that." Caroline pursed her lips and pondered how bizarre life could be. She turned her attention to Shelley's boyfriend at the time, a graduate student named Lucio Tokuhisa, who had been questioned in connection with the murder.

Shelley defended him. "Lucio would never have hurt Bonnie," she claimed. "He hardly knew her and also had an alibi. We were together that night and never left my apartment." She sighed. "I didn't lie for Lucio and he certainly didn't lie for me, in case you're wondering if I could've strangled to death my best friend."

The thought had crossed Caroline's mind, as jealous rage often proved to be a strong motivator for homicidal behavior. But she saw no reason to believe that was the case here. For now. "Thanks for telling me that," she told her appreciatively. "If only for the record."

"Is it true that Bonnie's brother, Lance, works for the Honolulu Police Department?" Shelley asked.

"Yes. He's a homicide detective."

"Interesting." Her eyes lit up. "Bonnie used to always talk—or actually brag—about her kid brother and how she planned to have a lot of fun with him when he came to visit." Shelley's expression turned sour. "I'm sorry they never got that chance to hang out on the island."

"Me too." Caroline was saddened that a killer saw to it that their plans were disrupted by tragedy. Bringing the unsub to justice would be the only positive to come out of this for everyone. Caroline handed Shelley her card, which included an office and cell number, and said, "If you think of anything else, don't hesitate to give me a call."

"I will," she promised.

They both stood and Caroline asked out of curiosity, "By the way, are you and Lucio still an item?"

Shelley laughed. "We were never an item. It was all about having fun while it lasted, which wasn't for very long. It was better that way for both of us."

Caroline couldn't help but think about her relatively short-lived relationship with Lance. It too was fun while it lasted. When it ended, for at least one of them, it wasn't better—it took her a long time to get over him. Did he have any regrets? "Mahalo for your time," Caroline told Shelley before leaving the office.

Outside, Caroline moved across the walkway lined with palm and cannonball trees, and spotted a couple of geckos chasing one another across the green grass. As she headed for the parking lot, her cell phone chimed. Removing it from the pocket of her knit pants, she saw that someone had sent her a text message.

Best to let sleeping dogs lie. Or you'll be very sorry.

Caroline gasped as she read it again. She had just been threatened by someone. But who? Instinctively, she looked around, but saw no one in particular spying on her. How had the person accessed her number? The text came from an unknown sender, who was apparently warning her off investigating the murder of Bonnie Warner. Could it be Bonnie's killer?

I better get out of here before I become a target too, Caroline thought nervously, and raced for her car while constantly looking over her shoulder as if an assailant would materialize at any moment.

Chapter Five

Lance walked into the Palms Hula Dance Studio on Kapiolani Boulevard, where hula lessons were underway for older adults. The slender green-eyed twentysomething instructor was Sarah Mankiewicz, based on her name and picture on a window display he saw before entering. When she saw Lance, she paused the lessons and headed his way.

"Aloha," she greeted him with a smile. She wore her long blond hair in a French rope braid and had on a red spaghetti strap top, grass skirt and was barefoot.

"Aloha," he responded. Then he flashed his ID and said, "Detective Warner. I'm with the HPD's Criminal Investigation Division. We're investigating the death of Jill Hussey."

Sarah reacted. "Why don't we go outside to talk?" Lance followed her through the double doors, before she continued, "I'm truly sorry about what happened to Jill, but I don't know anything about it."

"Her ex, Kurt Preston, says he was with you for the entire night during the time that Ms. Hussey was being killed," Lance told her. "Can you confirm that?"

"Yes," she said succinctly. "We were together. But just out of curiosity, why would you think Kurt would murder someone he was no longer with?"

"I wasn't accusing him," Lance stressed, "so much as eliminating him as a suspect. Intimates, including former, are typically looked at in cases such as this."

"Kurt isn't that type of guy," Sarah said, defending him.

"Maybe you're right. But just for the record, we don't always know people as well as we think we do." Lance could see that she was at least considering this. As it was, given that she had verified that Preston was with her when the murder of his ex-girlfriend was taking place, this would have to stand up for now. "I'll let you get back to your class," he told her.

"Mahalo." Sarah met his eyes. "Hope you find the killer."

"I will," he replied with determination, even while Lance wondered if it was the same unsub who took away Bonnie's world. And a good chunk of his own as a result.

Lance walked away and felt his cell phone vibrate to indicate a caller. He lifted it from his pocket and saw that it was Caroline, which immediately put a smile on his face. "Hey," he answered.

"Someone just sent me a threatening text message." She spoke in a harried tone of voice. "I think it may have something to do with Bonnie's murder—"

FIFTEEN MINUTES LATER, they were seated across from each other at the Coffee Times Café on Kalakaua Avenue, as Lance stared at the definitely ominous text message.

Best to let sleeping dogs lie. Or you'll be very sorry.

He gazed at Caroline's attractive face, detecting the concern in her expression as she sipped on an espresso drink. "Did you see anyone when you received this?"

"No one who seemed suspicious." She blinked. "But I had a feeling I was being watched, as if to see firsthand if I'd gotten the message."

Lance sat back and tasted his own latte. "Yeah, and that message seems to indicate someone is starting to feel very uncomfortable with your—our—digging into Bonnie's death and thinks intimidating tactics such as this will somehow make us look the other way."

"That's not going to happen." Caroline made her point clear with the snap in her tone.

"Not a chance," he agreed sharply. If they were beginning to make some headway into his sister's death, he would be damned if they would let up. Lance was happy to know Caroline felt the same way. That said, with this threat, he was concerned for her safety. He wasn't about to allow what happened to Bonnie to happen to Caroline. Not if he could help it.

"I don't suppose we can trace the text back to the sender?" she asked.

In noting that the text was sent anonymously, Lance said, "My guess is the person used a burner phone and immediately tossed it once done."

"Figured as much." Caroline lifted her drink.

"We'll check it out nevertheless."

"Not sure how the unsub got my number," she said.

"Could have been several ways," he replied, but suspected that the sender knew what they were doing in accessing her cell phone number. Meaning the unsub might be willing to take it a step further if the demand wasn't met.

"Still weird."

"You said you got the text after you left the office of Bonnie's friend Shelley Pacheco?"

"Yes," Caroline replied.

"You think she could've sent the text message?" Lance asked.

"Hard to imagine that. She seemed to really care for your sister and doesn't seem like the type who would want to scare me off from discovering who was responsible for her death."

"That's good to know. Never met her, but knowing Bonnie as I did, she seemed particular in who she chose to befriend. Shelley had to have been the right type of person to win her confidence."

Caroline tilted her face. "Shelley said that Bonnie talked often about her little brother and couldn't wait to see you in Hawaii."

Lance smiled. "That so?" He flashed back to that memory of their plans and only wished they had been able to see them through. "It would've been terrific as a teenager to hang out with Bonnie and her friends in Honolulu."

Caroline reached out and touched his hand. "I know." That small gesture moved Lance and he appreciated that it came from the heart. She removed her fingers and said, "Beyond Shelley, we can eliminate Bonnie's ex-boyfriend, Bradley Nolte, as a suspect in sending the text message or otherwise. Discovered he died a decade ago, the result of a vehicle rollover crash."

"Too bad for him," Lance said, though glad that someone Bonnie cared for at one point wasn't involved in a current attempt to impede the investigation into her death.

"I also have no reason to believe at the moment that Lucio Tokuhisa, Shelley's former boyfriend at the time of Bonnie's death, should be considered a suspect, as his alibi back then checked out."

Lance nodded. "Okay, Tokuhisa's not on our radar."

"So, we need to figure out who might be trying to scare me off," Caroline said, "before someone else is killed, assuming we're talking about the same past and present killer."

"Yeah, about that…" Lance sipped his coffee. "I heard that you spoke with Lieutenant Powell." He would have liked to have been in on the conversation. Though he and Powell had discussed Bonnie's murder, it had always been informally. Getting his take in a more official capacity as someone who had been there might have been helpful.

"Yes, I thought it might be a good idea to drop by and talk with him," Caroline said nonchalantly. "I also thought it would be good to do it alone as the lead investigator in this cold case. Didn't want things to be too awkward between you and your boss, though I understand he was the one who set reopening the case into motion."

Lance didn't argue the point, knowing she had been put in a difficult position in not wanting to cause any strife between him and Powell. Still, if they were to work together, he needed Caroline to know she could count on his support over and beyond anything else. Especially when it came to learning the truth about what happened to Bonnie. No matter the toes he had to step on. He relayed this to her in the softest tone, not wanting to drive any type of wedge between them in sharing information. Never mind the wedge he had created on the personal side in their relationship nearly three years ago.

"Understood," she said evenly, and lifted her cup as though needing a distraction.

"So, what did Powell have to say?" Lance was curious.

"He gave his take on the investigation into your sister's death and hitting a dead end, as well as thoughts on the current investigation and wanting to leave no stones unturned in seeing if the two were connected. That included going outside the department to ensure that there was no conflict of interest anywhere to impede progress in the case."

Lance had no issue with anything she said. Or Powell's perspective on the old and new cases. Made sense to have Caroline as the point person in pursuing the investigation. Was also nice having her around. "Just so you know, I don't fault the lieutenant for what happened to Bonnie." He needed to say this to her. "He did his job and came up short. It happens in this business. I also have to go along with his wanting to use your department to take on what we've been unable to get to the root of on our own."

She smiled. "Glad that we're on the same wavelength in moving forward."

"Me too." If that hadn't been the case, he would have made certain that they kept the wavelength between them as harmonious as possible.

"Regarding the latest ligature homicide," Caroline said, "how did you make out with Jill Hussey's boyfriend?"

Lance twisted his lips. "Apparently, Jill Hussey

and Kurt Preston were no longer together at the time of her death."

"Oh…" She gave him a thoughtful look and Lance couldn't help but wonder if she was thinking about their own breakup, something that was weighing on him more and more.

"Beyond that, he was too young to have been Bonnie's killer, which of course doesn't mean we aren't looking at two killers. In any event, Preston's alibi checked out."

Caroline sipped her drink, then said, "We'll just have to put our heads together and see if we can come up with some answers that can put both cases to rest."

"Yeah." Lance gazed at her and tossed out casually what had been on his mind. "So, where are you staying these days?" Last he knew, she had been living in a nice little plantation-style house in East Honolulu. Was that still the case?

Her eyes widened. "Why do you ask?"

Lance could pose the same question to himself. The answer would be twofold—mostly professional and partly out of personal curiosity—but he doubted she would see it that way. "I was just wondering for safety reasons," he said, giving a half-truth. "With someone texting you to back off the cold case, I'm concerned about your health and welfare."

Caroline's features relaxed. "I have a condo in Waikiki," she said matter-of-factly. "It's a secure condominium high-rise with a security guard. You need a passkey to enter the building and use the elevators."

"Good." *Check off one worry*, Lance thought. Still, he couldn't help but contemplate her moving from one place to another, but not with him. When did that happen? Once upon a time, he'd thought about asking her to move in with him or even somewhere else together. He'd been the one to scuttle that. So could he blame her for getting on with her life? But with whom? He'd already established she wasn't married with the absence of a wedding ring. Did that mean she was still available?

"Are you still in the same place by the marina?" she put forth questioningly.

"Yep," he admitted, as though that were a bad thing. "Haven't found a reason to move."

"Maybe just a change of scenery." Caroline hunched her shoulders. "I'm just saying."

"I can't disagree with you there. Change can be nice." Lance sipped on the latte thoughtfully and asked, before he could hold back the question, "Are you seeing anyone?"

She gave a sardonic chuckle. "Not that it's any of your business at this stage, but no, I'm currently single."

"You're right, it isn't any of my business," he acknowledged, even if it felt like he had been punched in the stomach. Had he truly expected her to wait around for him? See if he would change his tune and want to get back together? It didn't work that way in the real world. That wasn't to say he wouldn't jump at the chance to start seeing her again.

"But since you asked, what about you?" Caroline hit him with a straight look. "Break any other hearts lately? Or have you found *the one* and are sticking with her?"

"Ouch," Lance uttered, and feigned being physically injured. Clearly, he had hurt her and himself at the same time. As such, it was hard to push back and risk only making matters worse. But he at least wanted to answer her set of questions. "There is no one in my life at the moment," he said simply. "There hasn't been anyone for a long time or hearts to break." More specifically, he hadn't dated anyone steadily since Caroline, as Lance had been too absorbed in his own pity party and work to focus on the love and family that he wanted more than anything. He was sure Bonnie would have wanted that for him too. But was it too late to expect it? Especially from the one he had wounded the most by rebuffing the love she'd offered him?

CAROLINE ADMITTED TO herself that she probably should have refrained from the sarcasm where it concerned Lance and adding more women to the wounded-hearts club. What happened between them was over and done with. Wasn't it? It was what it was and beneath her to play the bitter ex-girlfriend role.

They were different people now. Weren't they? Yes, both were single and neither was looking to get involved at the moment. Certainly not with each other. Been there, done that.

She credited him for at least not swallowing the bait and dwelling on something she needed to get over. Even if his mere and very manly presence was making that all but impossible. But she had to try to stay focused on the cold case that had drawn them together. And for which she had sought his reassurance when receiving that portentous text message two hours ago.

From the coffee shop, Lance had followed Caroline to her office, where they managed to stay in the professional lane while going over the case file of Bonnie's death. They reviewed every piece of evidence. Every witness statement or recollection regarding the crime, before and after. Every observation and bit of information from law enforcement pertaining to the case. They studied the list of suspects in the murder. At the top of the heap was George Tacang. According to the report on him, he'd been working as a custodian at the apartment building Bonnie lived in and had been seen lurking around the complex after his working hours were over. But they did not find Tacang's DNA or fingerprints at the crime scene.

Then there was Kirsten Breckenridge, a hot-tempered, resident at the complex, who was said to have a run-in with Bonnie the day before that ended with

Kirsten threatening to come after her. She had an alibi for the time of Bonnie's death. So too had Raúl Hargitay, a homeless man who had been arrested for stalking, among other offenses, and had, according to witnesses, confronted Bonnie at least once when she refused to give him money. Hargitay had supposedly been panhandling in another part of the city when Bonnie was killed.

Caroline found herself coming back to George Tacang for some reason. With Lance breathing over her shoulder, she said, "They were never able to positively eliminate him as a suspect. Maybe Tacang did the deed and has hung around long enough to target someone else."

"I'm open to any possibilities at this point," Lance said. He touched her shoulder inadvertently and Caroline felt it reverberate throughout her body. "Why don't we see what Tacang is up to these days?"

She did a Google search for George Tacang, knowing that it might turn up empty, leaving them to try to track him down in other ways. Right away, she spotted a local website with the name George Tacang Custodial Services. Caroline clicked on it and saw the face of a Hawaiian man in his midsixties with short gray hair and a side part and gray-brown eyes.

"Does that look like him?" she asked, picturing the suspect when he was in his midforties.

"Yeah, I could see that," Lance said. "Pull up his photo from the case file."

Caroline did and it was apparent that, apart from his being older and a bit puffier in the face, they were looking at the same George Tacang who was questioned in regard to Bonnie's murder. "Let's see what the site has to say about him." She scrolled down. It listed the various janitorial services his company offered, including professional cleaning, window cleaning, antimicrobial cleaning, lawn care, emptying trash containers, general maintenance, consulting and more. Among the clients noted were commercial buildings and residential listings, including condominium and apartment complexes. "Looks like he's moved up in the world from his single-building maintenance days," she remarked wryly.

"Question is, what else has he been up to?" Lance asked. Then he said abruptly, "Stop! Go back up a bit." She scrolled back up the list of clients till he asked her to zoom in on one in particular. "The Cherrystone Apartments in Ewa Beach is where Jill Hussey lived and was killed."

"Hmm," Caroline uttered. "Tacang being connected with the apartments where both Bonnie and Jill happened to reside. Coincidence?"

"Maybe George Tacang can answer that for us." Lance's warm breath landed on Caroline's neck.

She lifted her eyes at him hopefully. "I think we'd better pay Tacang a little visit."

Before they left, Caroline opened her desk drawer and removed the department's standard-issue SIG

Sauer P226 9mm sidearm she carried in the course of her duties. She noted earlier that Lance was armed with a Glock 17 9mm Luger pistol, which he kept in his hip holster. As she tucked her weapon in a small-of-back holster, they headed out to confront the suspect.

CAROLINE DROVE IN silence as Lance stared out the window, caught up in his own thoughts as she was. They had some things to work through as far as their history was concerned and even their future, if such a thing were possible at this stage. But for now, she only wanted to concentrate on giving him some sort of peace in finding out who killed his sister and holding the person accountable. *I'll likely never see justice for my uncle's death*, Caroline resigned herself to thinking. But bringing closure to others was the next best thing. In this instance, she could only hope that Bonnie's murder did not go forever unsolved.

Caroline pulled up to George Tacang Custodial Services on Pohukaina Street. She wondered if it could really be that simple, that Tacang could quite literally lead them right to his door. They would find out soon enough.

"Let's see if this is the man who ended Bonnie's life," Lance said with asperity.

"Okay," Caroline agreed, and they left the car and entered the building.

At a small reception desk was a dark-skinned

young woman with brown hair worn in a center-part Afro. "Can I help you?" she asked.

"We're here to see George Tacang," Lance said stiffly.

She fluttered her lashes. "And you are...?"

"We're police detectives," Caroline answered firmly without bothering to present her identification just yet.

"Just a sec," the receptionist said, and buzzed him with the news. "He'll be right out."

Caroline saw a gray-haired man about Lance's height, but heavier, come into the lobby, wearing jeans and a light-colored shirt with the company logo. "I'm George Tacang," he said smoothly.

"I'm Detective Caroline Yashima, a cold case investigator with the Hawaii attorney general's Criminal Justice Division," she said, deciding to take the lead. "This is Detective Sergeant Lance Warner of the Honolulu Police Department. We'd like to talk to you about Bonnie Warner." *For starters*, Caroline thought.

She watched Tacang take a hard look at Lance, who held his gaze, and back to her, before he responded tonelessly, "Haven't heard that name in a long time."

"Haven't you?" Lance tossed the words back at him doubtfully.

Tacang rubbed his chin. "You related to her or something?"

"Bonnie was my big sister."

"I see." He took a breath, glanced at the receptionist then at Lance, before saying uncomfortably, "Why don't we step inside my office?"

They followed closely as the suspect led them down a corridor and into a corner room with modern furnishings and a picture window with a view of monkeypod trees. Without inviting them to sit, Tacang asked tensely, "What's this all about?"

"We've reopened the case into Bonnie's murder," Caroline told him. "You were a strong suspect in the crime at the time."

Tacang didn't deny it. "Yeah, tell me something I don't know. You people put me through the ringer for something I had absolutely nothing to do with. Reopening the case won't change that if you're hoping to try to pin her death on me."

"Only if you're guilty," Lance stressed, stepping closer to him. "You were seen prowling around the building while off duty. So maybe you decided to follow my sister up to her apartment and strangle her to death."

Tacang took an unnerved step backward. "I didn't kill her," he insisted. "I never even saw your sister that I could recall, till a detective showed me her picture. As for the so-called prowling, I often hung around after my shift ended in those days on my own time, just to make sure I had done everything I was supposed to do."

Caroline got between the two men. "Are you sure about that, Tacang?" she pressed him. "If you have something to confess to, it'll be easier on you if you tell us now."

"There's nothing to tell. I was cleared of any wrongdoing," he pointed out as though they had missed this somehow.

"With all the modern advances in DNA and other evidence in the commission of a crime," Lance told him, "if you are guilty, we'll find out this time and your freedom will be over."

"You won't find anything that incriminates me in your sister's death, Detective." Tacang squared his shoulders defiantly. "You're barking up the wrong tree."

"I suppose you're also saying you know nothing about a text message warning me off the case?" Caroline glared at Tacang. He held her gaze and looked confused, as if denying any knowledge of the text.

"We'll see about that." Lance sighed skeptically and Caroline understood that it was time for them to pivot from one case to another. "Another woman, Jill Hussey, was strangled to death two nights ago at the Cherrystone Apartments in Ewa Beach, which happens to be one of your clients," Lance said. "Know anything about that, Tacang?"

The suspect cocked thick brows. "Heard about it on the news. I had nothing to do with the murder," Tacang insisted. "Yeah, I get it. Seems weird that I worked with both complexes two decades apart. But that's all it is, a coincidence. Bad luck. Whatever you want to call it."

"We need more than just your word on that," Caroline pressed him. "Where were you on the night in question between eight and ten?"

"That's an easy one," Tacang responded, licking his lips. "I'm on a bowling league at the Aloha Bowling Center on Ala Moana Boulevard. I was there that night from seven to midnight. At least twenty people or more can vouch for this."

"You'd better hope so," Lance warned him.

Even with that not-so-veiled threat, Caroline sensed that George Tacang likely was neither Bonnie's killer nor the perp who took the life of Jill Hussey. But the first step in looking elsewhere would be to check out Tacang's alibi.

Chapter Six

As much as Lance had hoped that they might have found Bonnie's killer—and Jill Hussey's as well—in George Tacang, and put an end to a two-decades-long cold case turned hot again, Tacang's story checked out. Half a dozen members of his bowling league that they tracked down confirmed that he never left their sight during the estimated time of death of Jill Hussey. With no reason to believe they were covering for him, Lance had to accept that unless Tacang could literally be in two places at once, he was not the perp who fatally strangled the flight attendant. That flew in the face of the notion that one killer was responsible for the murders of Bonnie and Jill. But that didn't clear Tacang in Bonnie's death. As far as Lance was concerned, the man could have still strangled her and somehow managed to get away without leaving any scientific evidence to tie him to the murder. It happened.

But the pragmatic side of Lance had to believe

that, all things considered, Tacang was likely neither Bonnie's nor Jill's killer. That meant one or two unsubs were still out there, hiding in the shadows till exposed. Lance was sure Caroline was with him on that front as she sat musingly on the passenger side, as it was his turn to take the wheel in driving his official vehicle to the PD. Or more specifically, the Scientific Investigation Section, where they hoped to get some details on both the retesting of evidence originally tested after Bonnie's death, as well as what forensics came up with from the latest crime scene and Jill Hussey's body. Beyond that, Lance had an ulterior motive for driving. He wanted to take Caroline somewhere afterward where they could talk about them and hoped she gave him that opportunity.

For now, though, he was as content to stick with his own thoughts as she appeared to be, with both of them under pressure to deliver in their respective homicide investigations with more women potentially at risk. The fact that Caroline had been warned to back off by presumably the unsub who attacked Bonnie gave Lance cause for concern that her life could be in danger as well. He wasn't sure she was as convinced. But his gut instincts told him that the text message was no idle threat and, as such, needed to be taken seriously. Meaning they needed to either discover its source or crack the cold case of Bonnie's murder and nail the perp behind it.

When they arrived, Lance said equably, "Maybe forensics has found something for us to work with."

Caroline flashed a soft smile in breaking away from her reverie, which in and of itself intrigued him, and said, "They've been known to work wonders with little. That gives me hope that, combined with modern science, Bonnie's killer did not escape without leaving clues behind to help identify him or her."

"Me too." Lance left it at that and they got out of the car and headed inside.

The Honolulu Police Department's Scientific Investigation Section was Hawaii's sole comprehensive forensic laboratory. Lance couldn't imagine what they would have done without them when it came to solving cases that needed more than what basic police work could provide. They stepped inside the lab containing the Forensic Biology Unit and were met by Juliet Raju. The slender India-born criminalist was in her early thirties with brunette hair in a low side bun. She was wearing a white lab coat.

"Glad you two dropped by." She spoke cheerfully. "There's news…"

"Don't keep us in suspense," Lance said impatiently.

"What did you find out?" Caroline asked more gingerly.

Juliet sighed. "Well, let's start with the reexamination of the old evidence from the Bonnie Warner case. Whereas before we were really unable to get anything useful in terms of DNA that didn't belong to the victim or otherwise appeared to be corrupted, with modern advances in DNA testing, this time around we were able to collect workable DNA from someone other than Bonnie."

Lance's heart skipped a beat with the news and its potential implications. "Go on…"

"We have no way of knowing at this point if the DNA came from her killer or even someone investigating the crime," she pointed out cautiously. "Which is why we've submitted a sample to the Federal DNA Database Unit to see if we can get a hit with someone whose profile is in the National DNA Index System."

Caroline's eyes lit up. "And if there is a match, it may tell us who the unsub is in Bonnie's death."

"Yes, that is the hope," Juliet said optimistically.

Lance was still guarded in his own enthusiasm, used to disappointment when it came to solving his sister's murder. Could they have turned the corner in getting close to the truth? Then there was the murder of Jill Hussey, perhaps by the same perp, to contend with. "Did you come up with anything in your analysis of the physical evidence in the Jill Hussey investigation?"

"We're still working to see if DNA and fingerprints collected will point us somewhere other than the victim," she told him. "The prints have been sent to the Hawaii Criminal Justice Data Center to be analyzed. At the same time, we're examining the DNA from both murders to see if there is a crossmatch, which would strongly suggest the killers are one and the same across time. Keep your fingers crossed."

Lance allowed himself a grin. "Count on that."

"Good work, Juliet," Caroline told her. "We needed some positive news at this point."

"Mahalo." She smiled but warned, "It's too soon to know if we can give you what you need to solve the two crimes at once, but we'll do our best."

"That will have to be good enough for now," Lance said, thinking about the text message Caroline was sent earlier by someone hoping to derail one or both investigations. The attempt only made him—and Caroline—more committed to getting to the root of the murders of Bonnie and Jill. No amount of intimidation would deter them. No matter how much digging they had to do.

After they left the Scientific Investigation Section, Lance asked Caroline casually, "Do you want to grab a bite to eat?"

She gazed up at him tentatively. "What did you have in mind?"

If it were up to him, he would have loved to cook her dinner, something Lance had enjoyed doing when they were together. But they were no longer a couple and he had to respect some boundaries. The last thing he wanted was for Caroline to feel any pressure to step outside her comfort zone. Or was it his own insecurities at issue here in risking rejection after he had ended things between them two and half years ago? "I was thinking we could try a new steak and seafood restaurant on South Beretania Street called Aljean's Place."

"I heard they serve great food there," she said, smiling. "I'm game."

Lance nodded, knowing that the difficult part was yet to come.

CAROLINE HAD MIXED feelings about accepting Lance's offer for what amounted to a date. She wanted to believe that his only intention was to talk shop while putting food and drink into their stomachs, but she sensed there was more to his request. Rather than overthink it, which would cause her to pass on being in a somewhat-intimate setting with a man Caroline doubted she could ever trust again when it came to matters of the heart, she went with the basic fact that she was starving and didn't feel like cooking dinner. Ironically, Lance used to be pretty good at making scrumptious meals, she recalled, as part of his seduction maneuvers. Who else had he tried this on since they broke up?

She stared at him across the table as they sat alongside a floor-to-ceiling window with a scenic view. She ate a chopped salad along with a boneless Cajun-herb prime rib eye and downed it with water. Lance, who seemed deep in his musings, was poking at oxtail soup and a center-cut filet mignon. When he finally met her eyes with an unreadable look, he said with a catch to his tone, "I need to get something off my chest..."

Though unintended, Caroline found herself picturing his broad chest and six-pack abs, causing a stir within. "Go for it," she uttered with nervous anticipation and sipped from her glass of water.

Lance wet his lips with wine before saying unevenly, "I owe you an explanation for the way things ended between us two and a half years ago."

"We really don't have to go there," Caroline said half-heartedly. In reality, it was something she needed to hear, even if too little, too late to make a difference in their lives. Or to change what might have been.

"I think we do," he insisted and sipped more wine. "First of all, and this may sound cliché, it was never about you. Quite the contrary—you were terrific in every way. Smart, witty, sexy, ambitious, opinionated, a great lover and, obviously, gorgeous. Still are."

Though flattered by the compliments and eager to see where he went from there by way of enlightenment, she couldn't help but interject, "If you felt that way, why run from me—us—as if you couldn't get away fast enough? Did you get cold feet on the good thing we had?"

"No, it wasn't about cold feet," Lance claimed sharply. "I quit what we had because I wasn't in a very good place for sustaining it at the time. I was too self-absorbed with what happened to my sister and ultimately my parents, who died still grieving over Bonnie's unsolved murder; and the fear of losing someone else to commit to a relationship. Even when I knew you were probably the best thing to ever happen to me. So I bolted." His eyes lowered sadly. "Do I regret not handling things differently? Every single day. I screwed up by allowing you to walk out of my life by walking out of yours. If I could do it over again, I would've given our relationship a chance to grow as it deserved. I know that ship has sailed, but I just thought you needed to know where my head was at the time. And where it is today..."

Caroline actually felt a chill in hearing his heartfelt words. Even if part of her wanted to remain bitter at what he gave up with her, the better part felt appeased that he had given her a long-overdue explanation. She hadn't realized just how much Bonnie's death had weighed on him years later. And how this affected his ability to find love. If so, she would have helped him. Or sought to. But was he also saying he wanted to try to make it work again? Or was she misinterpreting his words? "I accept your apology, Lance," she told him sincerely, sticking a fork into her salad. "You did what you thought was best at the time. We've both moved on with our lives since then, so no need to rehash the past." Did she truly believe that? Or was it necessary to see what the future might bring?

"You're right, of course." He spooned the ox-tail soup. "I just wanted to clear the air that at times seemed thick as fog between us, with the hope that once this joint investigation is over, we could come away from it as friends at the very least."

"I'd like that too," Caroline admitted. The thought of them going their separate ways again was painful. Especially when the patter of her heart told her she still had strong feelings for him. And it sounded like his feelings for her were still there too. Did they dare act upon them? Turn familiarity and chemistry into hot sex without a safety net? But she didn't want to get ahead of herself and set up again for a fall. "Why don't we just get through this cold case and see what happens," she said, erring on the side of protecting herself.

"Agreed." Lance grinned while cutting into his filet mignon. He seemed perfectly content to leave it at that and let things progress between them at whatever pace she set, for which Caroline welcomed. She didn't want to put too much pressure on him or herself to move forward too quickly. Or recreate what they had before, if that was even possible. Was it?

Her rumination was broken when Lance's cell phone rang. His brows knitted with irritation, but he lifted it from his pocket anyhow, gazed down and said, "I should probably get this."

"You should," she told him, assuming it was probably important.

Caroline watched Lance's face contort as he listened to the caller before responding bleakly, "I'm on my way."

"What is it?" she asked, sensing bad news.

He locked eyes with her. "Another woman has been killed. Looks like she was strangled."

THE VICTIM WAS identified as Sophie O'Rourke, a thirty-year-old hairdresser in Makiki, an old neighborhood in Honolulu just northeast of downtown Honolulu. Her body was discovered by a coworker on the ceramic-tile flooring in the back room of the Kiki Hair Salon on Pensacola Street. Lance stood alongside Caroline and Detective Hugo Gushiken, studying what almost certainly was the latest victim of a killer whose reach might well date back twenty years. Unlike Bonnie, her short hair was dark and layered, but her skin was just as pale in death, aside from the discoloration around her neck. She was of medium build and wearing a brown salon jacket, black straight-leg pants and a wedge pump on one foot. The other was bare, as if her killer was intent on making a statement.

Lance turned away briefly, as Ray Kalember, a gangly bald-headed crime scene photographer, methodically snapped pictures to capture the decedent and potential clues into her death. Facing the victim again, Lance couldn't help but grieve all over once more for Bonnie and her all too familiar tragic end.

"The victim was apparently working alone when she was attacked," Gushiken remarked. "I'm guessing that the perp had been surveying the salon and waited till the right time before making his or her move."

Lance took a glance at a chair that had been knocked over, as well as some hair products that had fallen off a table. "Looks like she put up a struggle."

Caroline frowned. "It didn't do her much good against a more determined foe."

Though he was inclined to agree, insofar as the fate of the victim, Lance still believed it was possible she could help them nail her assailant as he noted what appeared to be blood on a finger. "Maybe she was able to come away with the DNA of her attacker," he said hopefully. "Or can otherwise provide some clues about the unsub even in death."

"A female assailant could have more easily caught Sophie O'Rourke off guard," Caroline said, speculating. "And, if so, even helped her to blend in more effortlessly in the perp's escape."

"Good point," Lance allowed. But while he certainly believed that a female was capable of getting the jump on unsuspecting victims by placing a belt around their neck, rendering them helpless, and strangling them to death, all in all he leaned toward the unsub being male. Especially if they were looking at the same person who murdered Bonnie. Apart from one woman who was suspected in her death and then quickly eliminated from suspicion, there was nothing in the case file that suggested the perp was a woman.

Thoughts of male serial killers who strangled their victims came to mind, such as Gary Ridgway, the so-called Green River Killer, another referred to as the Boston Strangler, and Samuel Little, whom authorities believe strangled to death at least sixty women and likely many more. In the current Honolulu ligature strangulations, Lance couldn't help but see a similar pattern and type of perpetrator. "A clever male perp, quick on his feet, could have just as likely snuck up on O'Rourke," he pointed out. "Or even cozied up to her, before turning on her."

"That's a sound counterargument," she conceded. "And more probable when considering the nature of death. Perhaps surveillance video captured the killer coming or going." Caroline looked around for a security system.

"Afraid not," Gushiken said, furrowing his brow. "According to the coworker, Rosemary Nobriga, the security camera hadn't been working for a while, which obviously worked to the advantage of O'Rourke's killer."

"Not necessarily," Lance said. "We'll check the video of surrounding businesses and see if anything shows up."

"Good luck with that," the detective countered. "It appears as though the perp escaped through the back door, which was open when I got here, suggesting the killer could have entered the salon the same way."

Caroline sighed. "Whoever is killing these women—whether one person or two people—is still human," she stated. "Humans make mistakes and eventually get caught. No matter how long it takes," Caroline added, and Lance knew she meant the twenty-year gap that Bonnie's killer had remained at large.

"You're right," he told her, gazing at the latest victim. "O'Rourke's killer will be caught, sooner or later." *Along with whoever murdered Bonnie and Jill Hussey*, Lance thought.

When Ernest Espiritu, the medical examiner, arrived, everyone parted to let him through, while trying not damage the crime scene. He wrinkled his nose. "Hate that we have to keep meeting under these unfortunate circumstances," he said sincerely, touching his glasses.

"Tell me about it." Lance made a face and eyed Caroline, who looked back at him. He had finally gotten a chance to get some things off his chest. She seemed receptive to his regrets over the way he broke off what they had. He sensed that she might even be open to letting him make things right between them by giving it another shot. Or was that only wishful thinking that was far from reality?

"What are your initial thoughts, Dr. Espiritu?"

Caroline asked anxiously, turning to the medical examiner. "How did she die?"

"Putting me on the spot," he said drolly, while doing a rapid examination of the deceased with his gloved hands. "Based on the condition of her neck and other observations, my preliminary assessment is that the victim was strangled by a ligature, probably a belt, much like Ms. Hussey." He took a breath and gazed at Sophie O'Rourke's bare foot, then glanced about as if looking for the missing shoe. "Hate to say this, but if you weren't going down this road before, it looks like you have a serial killer on your hands who apparently again took one of the decedent's shoes as a trophy."

"We've already been thinking in those terms," Lance told him and glanced at both Caroline and Gushiken. But this upped the ante even more, for now they knew that at the very least someone was targeting women today. And if that someone was the same unsub who killed Bonnie, there were now three victims. Which made Lance wonder uneasily if there could have been even more attacks over the last two decades that had managed to slip under the radar. And thereby go unconnected, giving the killer a free pass.

At home that evening, Lance asked himself the same troubling questions. The better part of him believed that a serial killer had not run amok on the island over the years undetected. Most such killers were not that crafty to camouflage their lethal actions for twenty years. The more plausible scenario, Lance believed, was that either Bonnie's killer had taken a pause in the action only to start up again two decades later, or someone wanted them to believe that. Or had chosen to follow in a killer's homicidal footsteps. Whichever the case, Lance sensed the connection between Bonnie's death and the latest strangulation victims was real. And it wasn't going to go away till both the cold and hot cases were put to rest.

He turned his thoughts to Caroline, causing Lance's heart to warm, as he stood on the lanai, a beer in hand and the humid air engulfing him. He wondered what it would be like to hold her in his arms again. To make love to her till the wee hours of the morning, as they once did with satisfying regularity. Could they pick up where they left off? Would she be willing to let him back in her life? Give them a chance to see just how far they could go now that the air had been cleared and he was ready to have a long and lasting life with her?

Lance mulled those thoughts over as he sipped the beer before heading back inside, where he would once again be sleeping alone.

Chapter Seven

"Heard that another young woman was found strangled to death last night," Vera Miyasato said, standing just inside Caroline's office.

While wishing she could say to her boss that it wasn't true or one big mistake, instead Caroline confronted it head-on, stating sadly from her desk, "Yes, Sophie O'Rourke was killed at the salon where she worked. There's every reason to believe that the same person who killed Jill Hussey killed her too."

"I was afraid that might be true." Vera came closer. "Didn't take long for the press to get wind of it. They've already come up with a moniker for the unsub, the 'Belt Strangler.'"

Caroline pursed her lips. The belt part hadn't been public knowledge. Meaning someone from law enforcement had leaked the information. This was usually because of the belief, misguided or not, that the more the public knew, the more they could help identify the killer, leading to an arrest. Caroline was more of the mind that they needed to keep the perpetrator at as much of a disadvantage as possible, so the unsub couldn't use the media to track their progress in the case. She seriously doubted it was Lance who tipped the press. Though she knew he wanted to see Bonnie's murder solved in the worst way, he was too much of a professional to risk compromising active cases for one from the distant past, assuming they were totally separate. Caroline was still on the fence in that regard. She feared that a serial killer might have been at large for two decades while managing to keep a low profile for the better part of it. But was just as accepting that they were looking at two separate killers, with possibly only one currently committing murders.

"So, how are we doing on the Bonnie Warner investigation?" Vera read her mind. "Are we talking about the same killer targeting new victims, or what?"

"Still too soon to tell," Caroline spoke honestly, leaning back in her chair. "Lance…er Detective Warner and I are trying to piece things together stretching across twenty years in relation to what's happening right now."

"I see."

She paused and Caroline could tell that Vera had hoped to have something more definitive in the investigation to perhaps pass along to her own boss, the Hawaii Attorney General, Maria Nishikawa. Or perhaps to Lieutenant Dorian Powell, who also had a vested interest. "We're making progress," Caroline sought to assure her.

Vera smiled. "Something has to give, right?"

"Yes, I believe so." Caroline smiled back, even while wondering if they were on the right track in solving Bonnie's death. Or merely going around in circles while a modern-day serial killer wreaked havoc in and around Honolulu.

"Keep me posted," Vera said simply, before leaving.

Caroline sighed and turned her thoughts briefly to the two cold cases she had essentially put on hold, while recalling Vera throwing the multitasking card at her when handing her the Bonnie Warner case file. One of the other cases involved a deadly home invasion thirty-five years ago in the State of Hawaii, where a member of the Honolulu Liquor Commission and her two preteen children were shot to death. At first glance, it did not appear to be a random act of violence, with signs pointing toward an organized crime connection and violations of liquor law, but it was too soon to tell.

The other case was not quite as distant, but just as compelling in its own way. It involved a former diplomat and his wife who mysteriously went missing after driving away from their Waikiki home fifteen years ago. They were never seen again. That was, until bones were unearthed during construction of a boutique residential complex in Honolulu County, which were positively identified as those of the missing couple. Both had been shot execution-style, giving Caroline food for thought in trying to crack the intriguing cold case.

But for now, she was laser focused on trying to find out who killed Bonnie Warner. With the latest ligature strangulation murder in the city that bore resemblance to Bonnie's death, Caroline understood that whether dealing with one or two unsubs, it was imperative that they at least put a stop to the current homicides that had taken away the lives of the two female victims before their time. Yet it was just as important to her that they crack the cold case involving Lance's sister. Though happy that he had finally expressed his regrets about how their relationship ended prematurely, Caroline felt that the only way they could truly get past this and potentially have a future beyond a professional one, was for Bonnie's spirit to be put to rest with her killer being identified and, if possible, apprehended.

That afternoon, Caroline met with Lance at the FBI Field Office located in Kapolei, a prosperous city in Honolulu County, twenty-two miles away. In light of the latest murder, they decided to pick the brain of FBI Special Agent Matthew Eleneki, a Hawaiian criminal profiler and renowned expert on serial killers. He greeted them in his roomy office. Standing tall at, Caroline guessed, at least six-five, he was in his mid-forties and solidly built, with brown hair in a military cut and intense coal eyes.

"Aloha," he said routinely, which they responded to accordingly, and shook hands, before being asked to have a seat. Caroline sat beside Lance in faux leather chairs, while Matt, as he asked to be called, sat in a white leather chair behind a big desk, with a picture window beside it. "I took a look at the case files you sent me," he said thoughtfully. "Interesting…"

"What's your take on the notion that we're dealing with one serial killer spanning two decades of murders?" Lance asked.

Eleneki leaned back in the chair. "First of all, I'm sorry about your sister. I know it was a long time ago, but these types of tragedies never leave you."

"I appreciate that." Lance put a hand on his knee and glanced at Caroline. She saw the pain in his eyes in remembering it as though only yesterday. "You do the best you can to cope with your loss."

"I understand." Eleneki tilted his face. "Well, I have to tell you, I think that in all likelihood we're looking at two different killers. No question that the similarities with the manner of death and the missing footwear lends itself to the possibility that one unsub is responsible for strangling these women. That being said, a true serial killer does not take a twenty-year break from the action and then start up again as if nothing more than a day in the park. For one, the perp would be two decades older and, as such, may not be as physically or even mentally fit to take on the somewhat strenuous nature of ligature strangulation. Or maybe the challenges of staying one or two steps ahead of modern detective work as a cold case killer warming up again." He smoothed an eyebrow. "As to the two-killer approach, it makes sense that a new serial killer would emerge and perhaps borrow some techniques, calling cards, and such, from past killers whom the unsub has become fixated on. Taking the victim's shoe to recreate the dynamics of a previous murder is a perfect example. I'm not saying that is the case here, but that old adage that imitation is the highest form of flattery could be what we're looking at."

Caroline thought this sounded reasonable. Especially knowing the nature of cold cases and how most unsubs who perpetrated such offenses preferred to keep them cold. Drawing attention to themselves by resuming their criminal behavior would not only increase the risk of detection, but also help authorities to close the original case. In both instances, it would mean serious jail time for the perp. That notwithstanding, she could imagine an older but still reasonably fit unsub who killed Bonnie deciding for whatever reason to let history repeat itself in going after new victims and letting the chips fall where they may. It made sense to Caroline as she considered the threatening text message she received from possibly the actual cold case killer of Bonnie Warner.

If nothing else, killers are always unpredictable, Caroline told herself, making them all the more dangerous. "I received a text message from someone," she mentioned to the profiler, "warning me to back off the case, or else. I think it may have come from whoever killed Bonnie." Or at least someone who had knowledge of the crime or current reopening of the case.

Eleneki reacted. "Do you still have it on your cell phone?"

"Yes."

He asked, "Can I see the text message?" She took out her cell phone and brought up the message, handing him the phone. Eleneki studied the text and read out loud as if to himself, "Best to let sleeping dogs lie. Or you'll be very sorry."

"We weren't able to track down the sender," Lance said, before they were asked.

Eleneki wrinkled his nose. "That would've been too easy," he indicated. "Especially when the objective was to frighten, not be caught doing so." He handed Caroline back the cell phone.

"So what do you make of this?" She gave him an attentive look. "Have we reawakened someone who would prefer the Bonnie Warner investigation remains closed permanently?"

"Or is the intent to simply throw us off the investigation into the current murders," Lance threw at him, "by linking them to a past crime?"

"Hmm…" Eleneki was thoughtful. "Have there been any other text messages?"

"Not yet," Caroline responded, putting her phone away.

"If I had to hazard a guess—and that's all it is for

the time being, with the cryptic nature of the text—
it does appear to be a warning of some sort to back
off. Question is, what are you being asked to back
off from?" He eyed her. "Are you working on any
other cold cases?"

"Yes," she confessed, "two others." She spoke
briefly about them.

"Well, the text message could be linked to one of
those cases," Eleneki suggested. "Or it could be an
intimidation tactic, designed to interfere with the
investigation you're undertaking. At this point, it
could go either way."

"Assuming we are talking about two killers here,
Matt," Caroline questioned, "what's the likelihood
that they are connected in some way? Such as a father passing on his bad seed to a son to carry on his
murderous ways?"

Eleneki grinned crookedly. "Ahh, you mean like
the bad seed theory or something to that effect?"

"Yes, I suppose." Not that she bought into a biological predisposition to homicidal behavior. But
Caroline wasn't ready to rule it out either. "Or, maybe
a son or other relative was simply seeking approval of
a killer by following in footsteps that is more a case
of family ties or environment than biology at work."

"Though some studies have been interesting in
showing a correlation between criminality and ge-
netics, most criminologists believe this to be a potential factor in some cases, but not the determinant

variable in the majority of violent behavior." Eleneki sighed. "As to environment and criminality, that has a much higher probability in terms of association in following one's footsteps, so to speak That includes being in the same household or workplace as a killer that you are aware of and are susceptible to such influence in your own criminal behavior."

Lance clasped his hands so tightly that Caroline wondered if it was affecting his blood circulation. "While that's fascinating, if my sister was killed by someone other than the unsub who's taken the lives of two women most recently, I still have no intention of allowing Bonnie's death to go unanswered. If that means totally separating the cases moving forward, I can do that. But not one at the expense of the other."

"I understand where you're coming from," Eleneki voiced sincerely. "I know it's personal where it concerns the death of someone close to you. I've been there, having lost a relative to senseless violence. The two cases you're investigating are not necessarily separate in terms of who's responsible. As I've indicated, there are enough threads of similarity that binds them in some way, shape or form, be it environmentally or otherwise. You need to keep that in mind while looking for the answers you both seek."

Caroline watched as the deep lines on Lance's forehead softened and he said, glancing at her and back, "We will. Given that my own primary investigation is the serial killer at large today on the island—be it the same unsub from twenty years ago or not—I can't help but wonder what the motivation or trigger was for the latest strangulations. Are we looking at merely a copycat or a continual killer? Or is there something deeper going on here?"

"I believe the current killer, regardless of whether or not the unsub is mimicking a past murder, is in fact making a statement of some sort," Eleneki replied straightforwardly. "Just what that is, we have no way of knowing until we get the person in custody and see what their intentions were, other than the simple thrill of taking a life and wanting more of the same."

Lance rubbed his jawline. "In Bonnie's case and the murders of Jill Hussey and Sophie O'Rourke, I can't help but wonder if the crimes were acquaintance or stranger perpetrated. The former makes more sense than the latter in the manner of entry, attack and lack of physical evidence."

Caroline brushed shoulders with him when she articulated rationally, "There's something called friendly strangers who are smart enough to get people to let down their guard as though an acquaintance. Or are opportunistic in taking advantage of easy access or lax security, before putting their plan into motion, including the expected getaway." At least she played on those thoughts in her head as it pertained to Bonnie and how she met her fate.

"The truth is, the unsub is equally likely to have

been a stranger as a familiar face, or vice versa," Eleneki explained. "Victims can be just as susceptible either way, depending on additional factors, such as witnesses, time of day, and risk of getting caught. Unfortunately, up till now, the rewards of killing have outweighed and/or justified in the head of the killer or killers the risk factor associated with both cases."

Caroline swallowed thickly, taking in the FBI profiler's assessment. She was sure Lance was also absorbing it as they grappled with unsolved cases twenty years apart. But while she and Lance were working together, they still had separate cases to solve at the end of the day. In spite of her ties to him and sorrow for the latest victims of a serial killer, Caroline's responsibility, first and foremost, had to be to Bonnie Warner and putting closure to the cold case. So, in that vein, she asked Matt, while already having thoughts on the subject, "If Bonnie's killer is back at it, why the passage of time?"

"Could be any number of reasons," he concluded. "The unsub may have been arrested for another crime and put away, only to be let out recently and resumed what he or she never intended to stop. The killer could've been unable to carry on with killing locally due to injury, a job transfer, romance, or progeny that was enough to distract from homicidal tendencies. Or the perp may have fully intended at the time to be one and done with it. But as time passed, got the urge to take another crack at it that turned into two cracks and so on, till the unsub's luck runs out."

"You left one out," Lance said. "Maybe the cold case killer has never really stopped killing. At least in the unsub's mind, where the first kill has played over and over before the desire to come out of retirement for real was too much to resist." His voice lowered. "Then there's the possibility that Bonnie's death was neither the first nor last time the unsub has struck, but for one reason or another, the killer has managed to stay under the radar. Perhaps more ligature strangulations or other types of homicides were perpetrated elsewhere."

"You make an excellent point," Eleneki allowed, and waited a beat, before continuing, "yes, it's entirely possible that the unsub—your sister's killer—may have killed again and again in an imaginary world. And even continued to kill on a real-life stage through the years without us making the connection or the unsub getting caught. But, in my experience, the latter seems unlikely. Serial predators tend to be creatures of habit and, as such, are unlikely to change their way of doing deadly business just to throw us off. Also, two decades is a fairly long time to serial kill without getting caught, no matter the modus operandi—though I know some killers such as Henry Lee Lucas, Robert Yates, and Lonnie Franklin, the so-called Grim Sleeper, have managed to buck the trend. And, as I said earlier, stopping for a long period of time and starting up again would be highly unusual for a serial killer for the reasons outlined."

Caroline bought into this counter argument, while imagining that Lance was mainly trying to cover all the bases. Or believed in his heart that his sister's killer was still at it as a serial killer, whether on a continual basis or stop and go, crossing two decades plus. For her part, she was still focused on the notion that Bonnie's killer could still be alive and on the island, even if not actively engaged in strangling women. But what if the perp only stopped for reasons beyond his or her control, but still had a serial killer's mentality? Caroline gazed at the FBI agent and asked, "If we accept that it's more likely than not there are two different killers, with your knowledge of serial homicides and its perpetrators, do you think it's possible that Bonnie's killer could have still kept a memento, such as her thong sandal, even if the killing stopped with her?"

"Yes, I believe it is possible that the success of killing and getting away with it may well have emboldened her assailant to hang onto a trophy shoe years later," Eleneki asserted, "enabling the perp to maintain some sort of perverse satisfaction, whether the unsub sought new victims or never killed again."

Caroline mulled that over for a moment or two, before another thought entered her mind and she put forth curiously, since he was the expert here, "Any chance we're dealing with a female unsub as a one-off in the cold case or the current case, or both, if committed by the same perpetrator?"

"Of course, there's always a chance that the perp could be a female for one or more combinations laid out," the FBI agent said without prelude. "Less likely for the latest ligature murders, though. Now that we've crossed over into serial killer territory, almost all serial killers, no matter the modus operandi, are male. Try more than nine of every ten such cases of serial murder. Now there are always exceptions to the rule, as evidenced by the fact that serial killers are not one hundred percent male, leaving room for some females to commit such crimes. Aileen Wuornos, Belle Gunness, Nannie Doss, Dorothea Puente, and Velma Barfield, for example, who acted alone in their serial kills, as opposed to a serial murder partnership."

They asked him a few more questions and Eleneki answered them professionally, before the meeting ended. "If I can be of further assistance in any way, don't hesitate to reach out," he told them dependably.

"We will," Lance said, and Caroline concurred, as they shook the profiler's hand again. She sensed that now that the FBI had been brought in on the investigation, their services would be helpful in trying to track down a present-day serial killer. As for the cold case homicide, Caroline knew that it was still largely up to her and Lance, with the backing of their bosses, to try and solve. No matter if the unsub had morphed into the so-called serial killer, the Belt Strangler.

IN MOSTLY SILENCE, Lance walked Caroline to her car, knowing Special Agent Matthew Eleneki had given them a lot to chew on. Beyond that, they each had their own thoughts on the cases they were handed and the pursuit of justice. The fact that they now had to contend with an official serial killer in their midst that went beyond speculation of a serial killer that stopped and started two decades apart, only complicated matters. But, for his part, Lance was not entirely convinced that there were two killers using the same playbook to commit their crimes, one in past tense and the other very much in the present. In spite of his reservations to that effect, he was in no position to dismiss this out of hand. Just the opposite. He needed to keep an open mind while keeping the dual investigations alive. Wherever this was headed, he was just as committed to continuing to investigate Bonnie's murder as the recent strangulation killings.

Also weighing on him was the baring of his soul to Caroline. Lance had put aside his reservations in speaking his mind and was glad he had. More than that, he was ready to make another play for her, knowing in his heart and soul that they belonged together. Did she feel the same way after he had broken things off lamentably two and half years ago, now that he had taken baby steps to make amends? Or had he burned his own bridges where it concerned having any hope of starting over?

"What do you make of Agent Eleneki's arguments?" Caroline intruded upon Lance's thoughts.

"For the most part, they're sound," he answered evenly.

"And what about the other part?"

Lance met her pretty eyes. "Well, even though it was important enough to get Eleneki's perspective on this, overall, I still believe in good old-fashioned police work on the ground to bridge theories with the facts of criminality. I think we need to proceed on the assumption that we could still be dealing with one unsub as much as two."

"I feel the same," she told him. "I think the text message likely has more to do with our current investigations—or at least the cold case—than anything else I'm working on. Which leads me to believe we're headed on the right course here."

"I'm with you." They neared her vehicle and Lance frowned. "Even with that belief, and taking absolutely nothing away from your skills as a cold case investigator or mine for that matter, we both know it's entirely possible that regardless of the desire, Bonnie's murder might never be solved." It pained him to think in those terms, but Lance had to be real about it. After all, it had been more than twenty years since he last saw his sister and the case had stalled for a reason.

Caroline faced him. "There are never any guarantees, Lance," she said laconically. "But there's every reason to believe this case is solvable. Apart from the enigmatic text message, our intertwined investigations with the victims linked by their missing shoes tells me that we're getting close. We owe it to Bonnie and the current victims of ligature strangulation to keep the heat on whoever is doing this. Even if it leads us in more than one direction."

"You're right," he said, feeling his confidence coming back in the belief that Bonnie's murder would still be solved, with her killer exposed and called to account. "I'm with you on this for as long as the investigation continues." No matter how long it took. He hoped answers were forthcoming sooner than later before more women had to die.

Caroline offered him a soft smile. "Deal."

It was in that moment he regarded her lips, which were perfectly thin and made for kissing. Having found them irresistible in the past, Lance felt a powerful need to kiss Caroline here and now. But he wasn't sure if that would elicit a slap of his face for overstepping his bounds as law enforcement officers on equal footing. Or be just as welcomed and wanted. The last thing he needed was to mess things up. Again.

While Lance was contemplating his next move, Caroline held his cheeks and pulled his face down to hers, whereby she kissed him. It lingered intoxicatingly for a long moment before she pulled back, gazed into his eyes, and asked boldly, "Is that what you were waiting to do?"

"Yeah." He blushed. "I have to be sure to add mind reader to your many charming qualities."

She laughed. "Go for it. But I have to admit, it was less about having a sixth sense than your body language."

"Oh, really?" Was it that obvious? He couldn't deny that she did things to him that his body couldn't help but react to. In spite of that, Lance tried not to embarrass himself again.

"Figured we may as well get that sexual tension between us over with," she said teasingly, unlocking her car. "Now we can get back to business. See you later, Detective Warner."

Taken aback, he watched as she got into the vehicle, started it, and drove off.

Chapter Eight

What was I thinking? Caroline asked herself, even as she spied Lance through the rearview mirror as she left the FBI Field Office parking lot. Did she really just kiss her ex-lover, ignoring all the reasons for not wanting to get involved with him again? How wise was that, with them still having to work together? On the other hand, she'd sensed that he wanted to kiss her just as badly, if not more, but hesitated just long enough, compelling her to beat him to the kiss. His mouth felt good on hers, Caroline had to admit, conjuring up memories of times gone by. Maybe it was best that they got it out of their system. Right? So, where did they go from here?

She put that thought on hold when her phone rang, as if to deliberately prevent Caroline from confronting still unresolved issues with Lance that had suddenly become more convoluted as well as enticing. With her cell phone in the car phone mount, she saw that the caller was Detective Eliza Taracena of the HPD's

Cold Case Unit. Caroline put it on speakerphone and said, while keeping eyes on the road, "Hey."

"Hey," Eliza responded. "Wanted to check in with you on the Bonnie Warner case. Been trying to catch up with Lance for some news, but we seem to keep missing each other."

"Sorry about that." For her part, Caroline definitely wanted to keep her fellow cold case investigator in the loop, even if the case had been forwarded to the Hawaii Department of the Attorney General, Criminal Justice Division. She brought her up to date on where things stood at the moment, knowing the case was still cold with more progress needed.

"I think I may have something for you," Eliza said enthusiastically. "I've been doing some digging on original suspects in Bonnie's murder. Good to hear that you were able to eliminate George Tacang as a suspect again in the current murder investigation. I was able to track down another suspect, Kirsten Breckenridge."

"Really?" Caroline perked up with interest. She hadn't quite gotten to probing into the current whereabouts of the temperamental, onetime drug addict who lived in the same apartment building as Bonnie.

"She's now Kirsten Vanderham and runs the Aloha Substance Abuse Treatment Center on Punahou Street."

"Hmm…" Caroline uttered, as she thought about

the woman's confrontation with Bonnie a day before she died.

"If you're available, I thought we could drop by there and have a chat with her," Eliza suggested. "If only for elimination purposes in the ongoing serial killer investigation in relation to the Warner case."

Caroline mused about the possible single kill female offender, as well as the female serial killer they explored with FBI Special Agent Matthew Eleneki. Could Kirsten Breckenridge or Vanderham be their unsub in both investigations? "I'm in," Caroline said. "I can pick you up in half an hour."

"I'll be ready. Mahalo."

"See you then." Caroline disconnected the call. She wondered if she would run into Lance while at the police department. If so, would it be awkward between them after the kiss? Or only make them both want to go further the next time, damn what it might or might not mean down the line?

As it was, they missed each other altogether, as Eliza had passed along that Lance was apparently in the process of interviewing a person of interest seen on surveillance video near the salon where Sophie O'Rourke was killed. Caroline could only hope that there was light at the end of the tunnel in the dual investigations, even as she tried to maintain a proper perspective when dealing with crime and criminals and the challenges put forth in solving cases.

During the drive to the treatment center, Caroline listened as Eliza droned on about her love life, or lack thereof, but remained convinced that she had learned from the losers and there were still good men waiting to be found. Caroline didn't disagree. Though still shaken from being burned by Lance, she also remembered the good times they had. Including the good feeling that came from the kiss that day. Seemed as though time was capable of healing all wounds. Had he turned over a new leaf insofar as being ready for a committed relationship, even if Bonnie's death was never solved? Or would getting back together with him only be the same old, same old, in setting herself up for a fall?

They entered the building, where a fair amount of activity was underway involving patients and staff coming and going. A medium-sized woman in her late fifties, with blonde hair and red highlights styled in an A-line bob, wearing retro brown glasses, approached Caroline and Eliza.

"Are you here for treatment?" she asked, glancing from one to the other.

"Not quite," Caroline answered, and lifted her ID. "I'm Detective Yashima of the Attorney General's Criminal Justice Division."

"Detective Eliza Taracena, Honolulu PD's Cold Case Unit," Eliza told her.

Though older, Caroline recognized the woman from the case file on Bonnie's murder. She asked

Get up to 4
FREE FABULOUS BOOKS
You Love!

To thank you for being a loyal reader we'd like to send you up to 4 FREE BOOKS, absolutely free when you try the Harlequin Reader Service.

Just write "YES" on the Loyal Reader Voucher and we'll send you 2 free books from each series you choose and Free Mystery Gifts, altogether worth over $20.

Try **Harlequin® Romantic Suspense** books featuring heart-racing page-turners with unexpected plot twists and irresistible chemistry that will keep you guessing to the very end.

Try **Harlequin Intrigue® Larger-Print** books featuring action-packed stories that will keep you on the edge of your seat. Solve the crime and deliver justice at all costs.

Or **TRY BOTH and get 2 books from each series!**

Your free books are completely free, even the shipping! If you continue with your subscription, you can look forward to curated monthly shipments of brand-new books from your selected series, always at a discount off the cover price! Plus you can cancel any time.

So don't miss out, return your Loyal Readers Voucher today to get your Free books.

Pam Powers

LOYAL READER
FREE BOOKS VOUCHER

YES! I Love Reading, please send me up to 4 FREE BOOKS and Free Mystery Gifts from the series I select.

Just write in "YES" on the dotted line below then return this card today and we'll send your free books & gifts asap!

➡️ YES ⬅️

Which do you prefer?

☐ **Harlequin®
Romantic
Suspense**
240/340 HDL GRS9

☐ **Harlequin
Intrigue®
Larger-Print**
199/399 HDL GRS9

☐ **BOTH**
240/340 & 199/399
HDL GRTL

FIRST NAME

LAST NAME

ADDRESS

APT.#

CITY

STATE/PROV.

ZIP/POSTAL CODE

EMAIL ☐ Please check this box if you would like to receive newsletters and promotional emails from Harlequin Enterprises ULC and its affiliates. You can unsubscribe anytime.

HI/HRS-622-LR_LRV22

her anyway, "Are you Kirsten Vanderham, formerly Kirsten Breckenridge?"

"Yes, that's me," she acknowledged. "I haven't been Kirsten Breckenridge for more than a decade, though. Mind telling me what this is about?"

"We've reopened the case into the murder of Bonnie Warner," Caroline said evenly. "Does that name ring a bell?"

Kirsten nodded expressively. "It's been a while but, yeah, it does ring a bell. Not sure how I can help you, though."

We'll see about that, Caroline thought, and said pointedly, "We're revisiting all the suspects in Bonnie's murder, which was similar to a current string of strangulation murders, in the course of the investigation."

"So, what are you saying?" She tilted her head. "You think I had something to do with these murders?"

"Is there somewhere we can talk?" Eliza asked bluntly. "Or would you prefer we do so here?"

Kirsten blinked. "Just a moment." She called over a tall African American male in his fifties with a gray Afro fade hairstyle and said, "James, can you hold the fort while I step outside for a minute?"

"Sure, no problem," he said, eyeing Caroline and Eliza with suspicion.

"Let's go," Kirsten directed the detectives and they followed her out the front door.

Caroline waited until they stopped by some bottle palm trees, before rounding on the suspect and saying levelly, "We just have a few questions for you."

"Go ahead, ask," she said edgily, "I have nothing to hide."

Giving her a direct gaze, Caroline got right to the heart of her suspicions. "In going over the case file in the death of Bonnie Warner, it came to our attention that you threatened Ms. Warner the day before she died. Care to tell us what that was all about?"

Kirsten sighed. "Nothing, really."

"Threatening to come after someone is more than nothing," Eliza pointed out, furrowing her brow. "Especially when that someone winds up murdered."

"You're right," she conceded. "I blame it on my drug use at the time. Bonnie and I got into an argument over something really stupid. I tossed a sandwich wrapper on the grass outside the apartment building. Bonnie saw me do it and griped about how it wasn't cool to litter. She asked me to pick it up like she owned the property. When I refused, she threatened to squeal on me to the apartment manager. That's when I threatened her."

"Did you follow through on the threat?" Caroline pressed her. "Like maybe decide to retaliate by breaking into Bonnie's unit and strangling her to death?"

"No!" Her voice rose. "It was nothing more than an idle threat while high on coke. I would never have actually done anything to her. I certainly wouldn't have committed murder over a stupid sandwich wrapper."

Admittedly, this did seem over the top to Caroline, even if she knew that some perps had resorted to murder for much less motivation. "Why should we believe you?" she asked nevertheless, and in spite of her seemingly solid alibi at the time.

"Because it's the truth," Kirsten insisted. "I actually hate what happened to Bonnie. Regardless of our differences, she didn't deserve to be killed, and at such a young age. I was getting high with a group of friends when the murder occurred. They all verified this to the police and didn't lie for me." She paused before continuing, "Since then, I've cleaned up my act. Been off drugs for years. I opened up this alcohol and drug treatment center with my husband, James, five years ago, wanting to help others fighting addiction like we were."

"Glad to hear that you've dedicated your life in this way," Caroline told her truthfully, knowing how devastating substance abuse had been to so many lives. Not exactly the type of person who was a serial killer on the side. Still, this was a criminal investigation, so she had to say it, "Last night, Sophie O'Rourke, a hairdresser, was found strangled to death at the salon where she worked."

"I heard about it," Kirsten cut her off, before Caroline could ask for her whereabouts during the esti-

mated time of death. "I was at the treatment center
all day and well into the night. Both patients and em-
ployees can vouch for this. It's not a nine to five type
occupation, but I wouldn't have it any other way. Oh,
and in case you're wondering, I have the same alibi
for the night the other young woman was strangled
recently by this Belt Strangler, as they're calling the
killer."

Caroline glanced at Eliza and back to Kirsten,
believing that she was innocent of both Bonnie's
murder and the latest killings, while still wanting to
check out her alibis, just in case. "Thanks for talking with us." As if she had a choice. "We'll let you
get back inside."

"Mahalo." Kirsten looked relieved. "I really hope
you find Bonnie's killer, even after all these years.
It's the right thing to do."

"We couldn't agree more," Eliza told her.

"No, we couldn't." Caroline shook Kirsten's ex-
tended hand, as did Eliza.

Before they could separate from her, a shot rang
out. It hit Kirsten, who went down involuntarily.
Caroline and Eliza crouched low instinctively, each
whipping out their weapons. Another shot was fired
at them, but missed, hitting the building instead.

"Do you see the shooter?" Caroline asked anxiously, straining her eyes to spot any movement that
might indicate where the attacker was and if the per-

son was approaching to get a closer shot. Her own gun was ready to fire at a moment's notice.

"No," Eliza responded unevenly. "The shots could have come from a passing vehicle."

"Or one of the buildings across the street." Caroline realized that they were pinned down and at the mercy of the assailant. She had no intention of being a sitting duck. She gazed at Kirsten, who was still conscious, moaning, and bleeding from the stomach. Was she the intended target? Eliza? *Or was that bullet meant for me?* Caroline asked herself, recalling the threatening text message. "Hang in there," she pleaded to the wounded woman. "We'll get you help."

"I'll call it in," Eliza said. "Cover me."

"Do it!" Caroline blared as she stayed low while aiming her SIG pistol this way and that, but saw no one. Even then, she was determined not to let her guard down, not wanting to give the perp an easy target.

Just then, a man burst from the treatment center and as Caroline pointed her weapon at him as a potential assailant, she realized he was unarmed and said he was Kirsten's husband, James Vanderham. Recognizing, he rushed to her side, oblivious to the danger that still lurked in the air like the humidity on the island.

As backup started to arrive and the threat lessened, with the unsub having apparently escaped, all

Caroline could think about was the eerie thought that she might have been killed before solving Bonnie's murder. Or seeing if there might still be a real future with Lance that he wouldn't run away from. Those thoughts were reinforced, along with the dread that accompanied it, when Caroline received another ominous text message that read:

It should have been you taking a bullet. Next time you may not be so lucky. Leave well enough alone.

THEY HAD PICKED up Raúl Hargitay, who was found prowling in and around the Kiki Hair Salon shortly before Sophie O'Rourke was murdered. Almost immediately, the name registered in Lance's head as one that had been embedded there for the past twenty years. Raúl Hargitay was the name of a homeless man who was suspected of killing Bonnie. A shaky alibi had been enough to get him off the hook, with the lack of hard evidence to the contrary. Gazing at the man across the table in the interrogation room, it was pretty clear to Lance that he was looking at one and the same between the past and present cases. Hargitay's mug shot, from when he was in his forties, was illustrative of his being in and out of trouble with the law for crimes that included loitering, criminal trespassing and disorderly conduct, and felony stalking. Now in his sixties, Lance peered at the lean man's weathered face. His thin salt and pepper hair was in a hipster cut and he had a matching yeard beard. He reeked of alcohol and body odor.

Lance resisted the urge to push his chair back a bit. Instead, he leaned forward and said directly, "The reason you're here, Hargitay, is that a surveillance camera picked you up loitering last night near a salon where a woman was killed. We're thinking maybe you had something to do with her murder."

The suspect yawned and griped, "I don't know anything about a murder."

Lance hadn't expected an outright confession. Not yet. Neither had Detective Hugo Gushiken, who was standing beside Lance and went at Hargitay verbally, "You sure about that? A witness reported seeing you inside the salon that evening, begging the victim, Sophie O'Rourke, for money. She turned you down, which the witness claimed caused you to have a conniption. Did you go back and strangle her to death as payback? It'll go much easier on you if you cooperate with us."

"I never laid a hand on the woman, I swear." Hargitay scratched inside his beard. "Yeah, I was pissed that she wouldn't give me a little change, but it's not like I didn't expect it. Most people never want to help out us less fortunate. I left the salon and went down the street, where someone was more generous. I never went back to look for trouble."

Lance wasn't quite convinced. He opened a folder and took out a photograph of Bonnie, one that had been provided by the family as part of the case file. Looking at it reminded him of how young she'd been when taken away. And how the cold case still grated at him. Sliding it in front of the suspect, Lance said, "This is Bonnie Warner. She was strangled to death in her Honolulu apartment twenty years ago. You were accused of harassing her for not giving you what she didn't have as a struggling college student. They weren't able to pin her murder on you then, but the case has been reopened. If you killed her in the same way Sophie O'Rourke and another young woman were murdered, the truth will come out and there won't be any hole you can crawl inside to escape!"

Hargitay studied the photo. If the common last name Lance shared when identifying himself to the suspect clicked, he didn't show it. Instead, Hargitay ran a hand across his mouth, and said thickly, "Looks familiar, but can't say I remember her face from this. I do recall the crime and being harassed by the cops back then, trying to get me to confess to something I didn't do. Kind of like now." He coughed loudly. "I didn't kill her, as I told the cops then. You've got the wrong man. Can I go now? I could really use a drink."

"Couldn't we all?" Gushiken mocked him. "We can't always get what we want, though. Especially in the middle of a murder investigation."

Just as Lance was weighing whether or not to cut

him loose in the absence of evidence strong enough to hold Hargitay, his cell phone rang. Lance took it out of his back pocket and saw the caller was Caroline. The kiss that she left him with earlier caused a stir, making him long to pick up where they left off. And go even further in reconnecting with each other on a carnal level. Something told him she wasn't calling for that reason.

Answering the phone, Lance was cut off immediately, as Caroline uttered unsteadily, "There's been a shooting…"

"What?" All he could think of was that she had been shot and was gravely injured. "Are you okay?" Lance knew how hollow that sounded, but he needed to know right now as his heart raced.

"I'm fine," she said with a sigh. "So is Eliza, who I'd gone with to see a potential suspect, Kirsten Breckenridge, in Bonnie's murder." As Lance weighed the name from the case file, Caroline continued, "Kirsten was hit…outside the substance abuse clinic she runs. I don't know her condition yet. We're on our way to the hospital. The shooter is still at large."

Lance was thankful that Caroline and Eliza were unhurt. But questions still rolled in his head. "Did you get a look at the shooter? Was Kirsten the target?"

"No to the first question." Caroline took a breath. "As to the second question, I fear that the bullet, and a second one that missed us all, was meant for me…"

Lance was certain she had good reason for believing this and said without prelude, "I'll meet you at the hospital." After hanging up, he stood and looked glumly at Hargitay, then to Gushiken. "Release him—for now," Lance said flatly, while believing they would know where to find Hargitay, if necessary.

Chapter Nine

It should have been you taking a bullet. Next time you may not be so lucky. Leave well enough alone.

Lance stared at the text message sent to Caroline's cell phone from an unknown person. "What do you think?" she asked him fixedly as they stood with Eliza in the lobby at the Kapiolani Medical Center for news on the condition of Kirsten Vanderham, who was in surgery. "Did Kirsten's shooter send the text?"

"It certainly lends itself to the possibility that this is the work of our unsub in the cold case investigation," he admitted. "Or at least the sender wants us to believe this, whether true or not. Since the shooting was on the local news almost from the start, it's possible, at least in theory, that the sender merely used this to his or her advantage in getting in our heads to try and get us to back off the case."

"Yes, I thought of that too," Caroline said. "Except that the incident occurred while we were interviewing the shooting victim and eliminating her as a suspect. But whoever shot her couldn't have known that, yet she was still shot in close proximity to me and Eliza. This tells me that one of us or both was the intended target."

"I agree," Eliza said. "Only the perp happened to either be a bad shot or was too busy trying to keep from being exposed to take better aim before firing off two shots and fleeing."

"We'll know more if and when Kirsten Vanderham can be interviewed again," Caroline stated. "But as of now, we have no reason to believe someone was after her and at that precise moment in time."

"You make a good argument," Lance told them both. "We'll see what forensics comes up with on the bullet removed from the victim and another that was dug out of the wall of the building it lodged itself into. In the meantime, we all need to watch our backs. It would seem that someone wants to keep Bonnie's murder buried forever, including the identity of the perpetrator, and is apparently willing to kill again to keep the secret going. That's assuming the unsub hasn't already returned to killing as a serial killer in the present."

Caroline's lower lip quivered as she said, "We won't know till we know. I'm thinking, though, that whether it's one or two killers, whoever killed your sister seems to be most intent on impeding our efforts. Which is why we'll continue to move forward and see where it leads and to whom—no matter the attempts to thwart the investigation."

"I'm with you," Eliza said bravely. "Whatever you need, I've got you covered."

"Same here," Lance voiced in accordance, knowing there was no turning back on learning once and for all, if possible, who was responsible for ending Bonnie's life. And maybe at least two other women. At the same time, he would be lying to himself if it didn't concern him that someone seemed to be gunning for Caroline. Losing her to a cold crime killer wasn't an option as far as Lance was concerned. Not when they had taken baby steps at reestablishing some kind of relationship.

When word came that the surgery was successful and Kirsten Vanderham was expected to make a full recovery, everyone breathed a sigh of relief. Lance agreed with Caroline that she needed time to recuperate before she could be interviewed. They decided to hold back as well in interviewing her husband James for any possible knowledge on the shooting, with spouses of victims usually at the top of the list of suspects, while other leads were pursued.

A few hours later, Lance and Caroline went to the Scientific Investigation Section to get information on the bullet that hit Vanderham and another that barely missed hitting her, Caroline, or Eliza; as well as a cartridge case that crime scene investigators recovered across the street. Lance hoped it would lead them to the shooter. "What do you have for us?" he asked the thirtysomething ballistics examiner, Alan Sheridan, who was tall and lanky with red hair worn in an undercut man bun, as they stood at his workstation.

"Enough to give you at least a running start," he claimed, "in closing in on the unsub." He put an image on his computer screen with a mostly intact bullet and another that was more mangled. "The bullets examined came from a 9mm Luger pistol. They were fired from a gun barrel with five lands and grooves and had a right-hand twist."

"What about the cartridge case?" Lance asked interestedly, taking mental notes.

"I was just about to get to that," Sheridan said, and switched images on the screen to a bullet casing. "The ballistic markings on the spent shell case are a perfect match for the bullet that was dug out of the building and taken from the victim. It definitely came from the same shooter."

Lance had gathered as much. "Any fingerprints on the ammo or cartridge casing?"

"Sorry, we weren't able to pull any prints from the evidence."

"Figures," Caroline moaned. "What about the murder weapon? Maybe the perp tossed it somewhere nearby, but left behind clues as to the shooter's identity."

"We're trying to help you there too," the ballistics

expert told them. "We've entered the bullet casing evidence into the ATF's National Integrated Ballistic Identification Network to see if there's a match with any other cartridge casings collected from other crime scenes that can be linked to weapons we recovered and test-fired to that effect."

"Hopefully, you can get a hit or we can find that firearm," Lance said, optimistic that the shooter could have slipped up and gotten rid of the gun in a hurry, hoping they would never retrieve it.

"Yeah," Sheridan said. "If we get anything, we'll let you know."

"Okay." Lance nodded at him and eyed Caroline, ready to move on. He waited till they were alone and said, "The fact that someone evidently decided to go after you makes me believe we're onto something in trying to connect the bullets to a weapon, which could presumably tell us who fired it."

"And whether or not the unsub is the same person who killed Bonnie," she finished the thought.

"Exactly." The desperation of the daytime shooting told Lance that the perp had to be running scared and had no qualms about taking Caroline out if she got too close to the truth. And anyone else who got in the perp's way, whether it was Eliza or Lance, which unnerved him. The thought foremost in his mind, aside from wanting to catch a killer on the loose for decades, was if Bonnie's killer had graduated to serial murderer, which would make the perp even more perilous.

"So we stay the course and see where it takes us," Caroline said firmly, breaking his reverie.

"Yes, absolutely," Lance agreed, understanding that the risks came with the territory in their profession, like it or not. "You hungry?" He'd noted when they left the building that it was after five.

"Haven't eaten since this morning," she confessed, "so I could go for some food."

"How about if I feed you with a home-cooked meal?" He took a chance that she would take the bait offered up.

"Hmm…" Caroline twisted her lips thoughtfully. "Just dinner, right?"

"You have my word that I won't try to pressure you into doing anything you don't want to do." Lance meant what he said. He hoped, though, that she might be ready to take things a bit further than their mouths pressed together earlier in the day. But he wasn't about to fight her on this, knowing that he had made his own bed, so to speak, and just might have to continue lying in it all by his lonesome.

"Then we have ourselves a dinner date," she declared.

"That, we do." He grinned. "You remember how to get to my place?"

She pretended to think about it, then responded playfully, "I shouldn't have much trouble finding it."

Lance was happy to know she hadn't forgotten. It gave him hope that Caroline remembered the good times they had there and could have again, if she only opened her heart up to the possibilities.

CAROLINE WAS ADMITTEDLY a bundle of nerves as she drove to Lance's house in Hawaii Kai, after going back to her condo for a shower and change of clothes. She had chosen a burgundy-colored cap sleeve sheath dress and black dress sandals for the occasion, while wearing her hair down. Though it was only dinner, or so he said, part of her wanted it to be more. She liked the feel of his hard mouth on hers that morning, even if it brought Caroline back to their history, which she had sworn not to repeat. But they were both different people today, right? Should she really judge him by the past any more than she wanted to be judged by an earlier version of herself? Maybe they needed to start with a clean slate and pretend he hadn't broken her heart once upon a time. Or at least, she hoped, as adults they could simply enjoy each other's company away from the stresses of their dual track investigations.

Caroline was able to reach her destination easily enough, even if she hadn't set foot inside Lance's waterfront home in more than two and a half years. How could she have forgotten what once seemed like it would become a shared residence? She wondered how many other women he had invited over—and had stayed the night? *None of my business*, Caroline told herself. After all, they were no longer together and he didn't owe her anything. Or did he?

She only rang the doorbell once, before the door opened and Lance stood there, a big grin on his handsome face. "Hey. Right on time."

"Being late isn't in my DNA", she reminded him cheerfully.

"I can see that." He laughed. "Come in." Caroline stepped inside and Lance, peering at her, said admiringly, "You clean up nicely. Great to see your hair down."

"Mahalo." Blushing, she gave him the once over and saw that his hair was freshly washed and he had changed into a gray print dress shirt, black chino pants, and gray boat shoes. "You're not so bad yourself," she told him sincerely.

"Thanks. I wanted to make myself at least presentable when having dinner with a gorgeous woman."

"Oh, really?" Caroline flashed him a teasing look. As far as she could tell, he was always presentable and good looking, no matter what he was wearing. But she was sure he already knew that.

"That way, if the food falls flat, maybe that will help mitigate the damage," Lance said with a chuckle.

She couldn't help but chuckle too at the absurdity of it all. "I doubt that you've lost your touch in the kitchen."

"We'll see about that," he teased her.

Caroline took a glance around at the layout and furnishings, and a sense of familiarity hit her, right down to the scent of masculinity that came with the place Lance called home. "I see you haven't changed much in the past two and a half years," she remarked, while wondering if this was true as well in his bedroom.

"Some things are best left as they are." Lance gazed at her meaningfully, giving Caroline the distinct impression there was a double meaning attached to the words. "In the case of the house, I'm satisfied that it has everything I need insofar as material items, access to the marina and general comfort level."

"Happy to hear that." Caroline tried to read between the lines as to what was clearly missing in the equation—a romantic partner to share his place and life with. Or was she overreading things? She spotted a small gecko climbing the wall.

Lance got her attention. "Why don't I get you a glass of wine and you can make yourself at home while I finish things in the kitchen."

"Or I can assist you in the kitchen," she suggested in an accommodating tone. "It would make me feel useful and help to reacquaint myself with the surroundings." Caroline wondered if she had just gone overboard in acting as if she belonged, in spite of how things ended between them.

"You drive a hard bargain," he said, grinning sideways. "Feel free to pitch in. The wine's in the fridge, goblets in the...well, I'm sure you can manage to find your way around."

"Good." She accepted the challenge, wanting the get together away from work to be as fun and relaxed as possible.

Twenty minutes later, Caroline sat across from Lance at the glass dining room table eating chicken katsu, a Japanese dish with fried chicken and panko bread crumbs. It was one of her favorite dishes that Caroline's mother often made for dinner. The fact that Lance remembered this, having prepared it together when they were dating, left an impression upon her. Maybe he really had retained much of what he felt for her then. Or at least in his cooking skills that included noodle soup, and tomato salad, served with multigrain bread.

"So, how did I do?" Lance asked, sipping on white wine amusingly. "Did I pass the palate test?"

Caroline chuckled, while eating the chicken katsu. "With flying colors," she proclaimed.

"Just checking." His eyes twinkled. "I don't do much cooking these days."

"And why is that?" She eyed him curiously, assuming work was the answer.

"Haven't had anyone in my life to want to cook for in a long time," he confessed candidly. "Maybe that will change."

"Maybe," she said without giving it much thought, aside from enjoying the meal and the company.

Lance sat back. "So, when was the last time you were on one of the other islands?"

"Earlier this year, I was on Maui as part of an investigation." She nibbled on a slice of bread. "How about you?"

"I went to Kauai this summer, also while working a case." He waited a beat, then asked, "When were you last on the mainland and where?"

"Last year, I visited my college roommate, who lives in Tennessee. The year before, I was in New York for a week." It was after they had broken up and she felt she needed to get away to an entirely different setting. Caroline chose not to reopen that can of worms. Not tonight.

She was thankful that Lance didn't seem to consider the timing of the New York trip. Instead, he said coolly, before she could ask, "A year ago, I let a buddy of mine, who works for the Idaho Department of Fish and Game, talk me into taking a short vacation for some R&R at his ranch in Boise."

"How did you like it there?" she wondered, imagining him as a rancher.

"It was an experience, that's for sure." Lance laughed while spooning noodle soup. "Enjoyed some fishing, riding a horse and checking out the terrain, but I'm much more at home these days on Oahu."

"Same here," Caroline concurred and tasted her

wine. Both had seemingly gone out of their way to keep the conversation light and not talk about their history or current investigations. She welcomed the respite, glad she decided to accept his invitation for dinner.

"Why don't we step out on the lanai," Lance suggested a few minutes later, with the meal finished.

Caroline smiled. "Good idea." They rose and brought their wineglasses with them. "I'd forgotten what a magnificent view you have out here of the Koko Marina at night."

"It's even better when it's a clear day and you can see the Koolau Range," he reminded her.

"Yes, I remember," she said wondrously.

Lance nodded. "Some things you just never forget."

Caroline lifted her eyes. "Such as?"

"Such as how good it felt to kiss you."

"Oh, really?" Her lashes fluttered expectantly. "And how good was it?" She remembered their kiss earlier that day.

"Very, very good," he contended, and took her glass, setting it and his own on a square eucalyptus hardwood table. Then, gently cupping her cheeks, Lance planted a soft kiss on Caroline's lips, deepening it as she made it clear by kissing him back that it was with her approval. When he pulled away, he uttered, "Seems like we went down this road a little while ago, only cementing how good it feels to taste your lips right now."

"Probably the same way it feels to taste yours," Caroline confessed, as a hunger built up inside to do more of the same. This time, she initiated the kiss, raising her chin and, after grabbing him, opened her mouth wide, before fitting it against his hard lips perfectly. She could taste his wine, causing her to feel even more intoxicated with desire as they made out like teenagers. But then the hesitancy kicked in and Caroline wondered if this was too much, too soon. So she brought the scintillating kiss to a screeching halt. "I should probably go," she said tonelessly.

"Or…you could stay," Lance countered in a pleading voice.

Caroline could feel her heart pounding. "What about the no pressure pledge?"

"Oh, that." He sucked in a deep breath. "Guess that was more wishful thinking that we'd somehow turned the corner. My bad. A deal is a deal. No pressure. I'll walk you out."

It was only after they stepped back inside the house that Caroline realized she was her own worst enemy where it concerned Lance. Why shouldn't she take a chance by giving in to her feelings of wanting to be with him? Living in the past was not healthy. He wanted her as much as she did him. They owed it to each other to take advantage of the moment and not seek more than the other may have been willing to give.

Before they could get to the door, Caroline turned to Lance and said ardently, "That won't be necessary. I think I'd like to stay."

He caught her gaze. "Are you sure?"

"Yes," she admitted. "I want you to make love to me, Lance." Even as she blurted out the words, Caroline wondered if it would be as passionate as before. Or might the wind have gone right out of the sails as far as how they reacted to each other in bed? She was about to find out.

"You've got it," he said in a snap. "Especially since I want to make love to you every bit as much, if not more."

"Then we're in agreement." Caroline was shameless in wanting the man and what he brought as a lover. Or at least what she remembered that had her practically seeing stars for days afterward. "Do you have protection?" she thought to ask.

"Yes. We're covered there, no pun intended."

"Okay." Caroline did want to have children someday, when the time was right. For now, though, she only wanted to be with Lance. Taking his hand, she guided them to the large owner's suite. Her eyes adjusted to the semidarkness, as an awareness swept over her in glancing at the retro bedroom furnishings, before homing in on the vintage king-sized bed.

Imagining them being on it again, Caroline turned to Lance and they kissed again passionately.

They stopped long enough to strip naked and check each other out. Caroline gasped at Lance's muscled body and erection and blushed as he admired her from head to toe. "You're stunning," he said point-blank.

"You are too," she returned unabashedly.

Lance disappeared briefly into the bathroom and returned with the condom. He climbed into bed, where Caroline awaited beneath the chenille bedspread and atop the soft sheet, with a ceiling fan spinning about. Her pulse raced with excitement, which grew to a fevered pitch as they resumed kissing, and Caroline's body reacted to Lance's touch. She touched him too, igniting an equal bodily reaction. Normally, she would have wanted this to be slow and sensual, enjoying each and every undulating second. But the needs and stimulation were too great to resist having him inside her now, in spite of Lance's apparent desire to the contrary.

"I can't wait any longer," Caroline cooed urgently. "Please… Lance—"

"If you're ready, then let's make love," he told her raspy-voiced, sandwiching himself between her legs.

The moment he entered her, filling her with his manliness, Caroline reached the point of no return, clinging to Lance for dear life, arching her back to meet his deep thrusts halfway. Almost simultaneously, his body quivered wildly atop her and Lance moaned with his powerful release. Tingling right down to her toes, Caroline knew then that they would need to go at least one more round to complete what they had started. Or just maybe never quite finished two and a half years ago.

Chapter Ten

Lance drank in the sight of Caroline, as low light coming from the en suite was more than enough to cut through the darkness in the room and illustrate just how gorgeous she still was naked. The beauty of her face and complexion notwithstanding, he was just as taken with the small perfectly rounded breasts, taut body from head to toe and natural scent with a tad of a floral fragrance. His libido was in overdrive with desire. The fact that they had just made love that lasted only long enough to release pent-up needs did little to crave his wanting much more of her. Having thrown their earlier relationship away, missing out on two and a half years of love-making and emotional support, was something he would have to live with.

But Lance was determined to try to make up for lost time and get Caroline back. Being together here now was certainly a good step in the right direction. He could only hope that her own desire for him would remain strong even after the hot sex and she would give him a chance to prove himself worthy of being with him again, over and beyond their sexual chemistry. At the moment, though, that was front and center, as Lance uttered wantonly, "What do you say we do a replay of what just happened. Only do it right this time?"

"I want that." Caroline reached out for him. "Let's make love, slowly and surely."

That prompting was all he needed for Lance to slip into another condom and proceed to show some patience while using his nimble fingers to caress her wherever she wanted, and then some. Caroline guided his hands accordingly, her breathing heightened with each stroke. She followed his lead in making her own hands magical in feeling him while wandering deliberately. Lance enjoyed the stimulation as he brought his mouth upon hers for a passionate kiss that had their tongues searching one another as if for a buried treasure.

By the time they discovered it, Lance had pulled Caroline onto him, lowering her so that they were locked together in perfect harmony as the sex sizzled. He easily flipped her over without breaking stride and with her legs wrapped around his back, they took their sweet time making love at their own pace. When the moment came for them to reach a peak of satisfaction, they soared high together, bodies slickened, heartbeats erratic, and the sounds of their sex ringing through his ears, while Lance held Caroline tightly until they were able to come back down to ground level.

"Wow," Lance said, still trying to catch his breath as he lay beside her. "That was amazing. No, you were amazing!"

"I could say the same for you." Caroline giggled. "You haven't lost any of your skills in bed."

He accepted the flattery as a good sign. "It helps when you have a partner who really turns you on and is just as skillful at making things click."

"I try my best," she spoke humbly.

"Which, in my book, is more than sufficient," he told her, and snuggled against her body.

"Good response." Caroline lifted her chin and they kissed. "I don't know about you, but I'm pretty exhausted."

Lance chuckled. "After what took place over the last hour plus, I'm not surprised."

She laughed blushingly. "So, just hold me and let's get some sleep, okay?"

"Okay." Admittedly, he too was tired and more than ready to sleep through the night in the same bed with her. And if, in the wee hours of the morning, the spirit moved them to kick into sexual gear again, he would be up for that too.

Lance fell asleep, but not before it crossed his mind that beyond the ecstasy of mind-blowing sex, he and Caroline were still in the middle of criminal investigations that had at least three women dead by strangulation across two decades. With that hanging over them like dark cumulous clouds, there would be no true rest for the weary until the cases were solved.

CAROLINE WAS CAUGHT in dreamland, where she and Lance were in a committed relationship and everything was right with the world, when a sound came from nowhere, snapping her out of it. She opened her eyes to the morning light and realized the sound was Lance's snoring. It was low, but steady. She didn't remember him as a snorer. Was this new? Could their blazing sex last night have something to do with it?

If so, I could probably get used to it if we're going to continue to make love, Caroline mused, coloring at the thought. As it was, she had no idea what to make of sleeping with the man who dumped her in their previous involvement. Other than that, they had needed each other after some trying times and made the most of the opportunity afforded them to do something about it. But beyond that, she wasn't sure it was a good idea to get too emotionally tied to him after one night in bed, as incredible as it was.

"Good morning," Lance said, having awakened, grinning at her with his hands behind his head.

"Aloha kakahiaka," Caroline said back in Hawaiian. They were both still naked beneath the sheets.

"Sleep well?"

"Yes," she admitted, suppressing a grin in remembering who woke her.

He sat up, rubbing his eyes. "Why don't I make you breakfast?"

Though tempting, Caroline wasn't sure that was such a good idea. "Thanks, but I need to go. A cup of coffee would be good, though," she said, allowing for more than just a hasty exit.

"All right." Lance forced a smile. "Coffee it is."

Fifteen minutes later, they were both dressed and standing in the kitchen holding their mugs of steaming coffee. Though Lance had returned to his standard detective attire, Caroline was still wearing her woman on a hot date outfit till she could return to her condo to change clothes. She recalled once keeping extra clothing at his place and vice versa when they were together. But that wasn't exactly the case in the present situation, was it?

"So, what about us?" Lance asked in a forthright tone of voice, as if reading her mind.

Caroline batted her lashes innocently. "What about us?"

"Well, if last night was any indication, I think we need to talk about where we might go from here."

"We had sex, Lance, as consenting adults," she stated. "It's probably best not to try to read too much into it."

He moved closer. "We're good together, Caroline. Maybe we should give this another try?"

Her eyes widened. While the notion had its appeal, the risks versus rewards of opening up her heart again scared Caroline. "I don't think we should rush into anything," she countered and sipped the coffee. "Between the cases we're working on and the way things ended between us before—"

She was stopped as Lance kissed her, causing Caroline's knees to buckle and her train of thought to become disoriented. "We owe it to ourselves to at least try," he insisted.

She touched her swollen lips while remaining resistant. "Didn't we go down that road before? You kicked me to the curb, Lance."

"I know." He wiped his mouth. "I've explained that. I thought you understood."

"I do," she conceded. "You were going through some stuff between your sister's death and other things. I get it. But I went through a lot too." Maybe he hadn't looked at it enough from her point of view. "I can't allow myself to get too emotionally attached to you again, only to have history repeat itself."

"That won't happen." Lance ran his hand along her cheek. "I won't let it."

"So you say." Caroline favored him with a skeptical frown. "Let's not rush into anything. If we're meant to be back together, it will happen. If not, we won't have any regrets." Could she really never regret not having a life with the man she fell for two and half years ago and was still in love with?

Lance's lips were pursed as he said, "If you really feel that way, I have to respect it."

"I'm not sure how I feel," Caroline stretched the truth. "This is just how it needs to be." She wondered how long she could hold out from wanting to be with him in every way possible. Or would he simply turn and walk away like before, without fighting to convince her that they truly did belong together?

When her cell phone rang, Caroline grabbed it off the travertine countertop. The caller was Shelley Pacheco, Bonnie's best friend. Answering it on speakerphone, Caroline said, "Hello, Shelley."

"Hi, Detective Yashima. I heard about the shooting that took place yesterday at the substance abuse treatment center and saw that you were involved. Are you all right?"

"Yes, I managed to dodge a bullet or two." Caroline glanced at Lance, who was sipping coffee and just as curious as she was about the call. "Thanks for asking."

"Don't ask me why, but somehow that triggered a memory regarding Bonnie's death that never seemed really important. Till now." Shelley paused. "Do you think we could meet?"

"Of course," Caroline responded eagerly. "When and where?"

"I have a break between classes at ten thirty. I can meet you then at the Akers Grill on campus on Maile Way."

"I'll be there." Caroline looked at Lance, while

noting that it was currently seven thirty in the morning. "Oh, and by the way, I'll bring along Bonnie's brother, Detective Sergeant Lance Warner. He's also working the cold case."

"That's fine," Shelley told her. "It will be nice to finally meet him."

"See you then," Caroline said, and disconnected.

"What's that all about?" Lance wondered. "Triggered memory about what exactly?"

"Your guess is as good as mine. Hopefully, she's remembering something that can lead to a killer." She lifted her coffee mug and tasted the drink contemplatively. "We'll find out soon enough."

"You look just like Bonnie," Lance was told by Shelley Pacheco as they stood in the café. He remembered her, if only from a photograph that his sister had emailed him of them. "Or at least the general features she had."

"Thanks," he said, having often been told that they had the same shade of eyes, type of nose and jawline. He wore that badge with honor, happy to be able to carry on a small part of Bonnie in his very being, albeit with a virile edge. This had served him well through the years as a so-called chip off the old sibling block, each of which had elements of their parents' physical characteristics.

"Wish we'd been able to meet back then," Shelley said, touching her glasses.

"Me too." Lance wondered what trouble he might have gotten into hanging out with his sister's older friends. Moreover, he wished to hell he had been around when Bonnie was attacked and able to defend her.

"Why don't we sit down," Caroline said coolly, looking from Lance to Shelley.

As they sat around the small table, Lance couldn't help but think about where Caroline left things between them. After the night of hot sex and his wish to build upon it, he wasn't sure where they went from there. Other than believing that they belonged together and he needed to work harder to get her to see this.

They ordered milk teas and Lance's focus returned to Shelley Pacheco. He waited eagerly to hear what Bonnie's friend had to say about her murder.

Shelley said gingerly, "Ever since you came to see me, Detective Yashima, Bonnie's death has been on my mind." She hesitated, tasting the drink. "It's been painful having to relive it, but with the case reopened, I didn't want to lose the opportunity to try to help in any way I could."

"What can you tell us?" Lance pressed her. "Do you remember something that happened?"

"You said a memory was triggered that didn't seem important at the time," Caroline reiterated. "What was it?"

"It had to do with the man Bonnie had been dating," Shelley said.

"You mean Bradley Nolte?" she asked and sipped the milk tea. Lance thought about the guy his sister called her boyfriend, till he broke her heart by cheating on her. But their relationship supposedly ended months before Bonnie was murdered. Nolte had an alibi for the time of the crime. Could he have played the investigators?

"No," Shelley uttered, glancing out the window. "After Bonnie and Bradley broke up, she started seeing an older man named Frank. That is, till she discovered he was married and ended things."

Lance peered at her. "You think he might have had something to do with Bonnie's death?"

"I don't know. Maybe. I remember Bonnie telling me that he didn't seem to want to take no for an answer, as far as her walking away from his extramarital affair." She wrung her hands. "What came back to me was I remembered thinking after Bonnie's death that the lead investigator in the case, a Detective Roger Nielsen, looked a lot like Frank. I only met him once when Bonnie and I went out to a club and there he was. He came over to us, was handsome and charming, and went straight for Bonnie. She was hooked right away, and they started dating. I had more or less put the entire thing out of my memory."

"Are you telling us that you believe that this Frank

was in fact Detective Roger Nielsen?" Caroline asked, a catch to her voice, as she gazed at Lance and back. "Maybe Nielsen just looked like him."

Shelley fidgeted. "I can't say for certain," she hedged. "Still…"

Lance stiffened. "That's a serious allegation to even suggest that the lead investigator in my sister's death may have actually killed her." He clenched his jaw as he considered the implications. "Is that what you're telling us?"

"I don't know what I'm saying." Shelley jutted her chin nervously. "Or maybe I do." She took a breath. "With the image of Frank resurfacing in my mind, juxtaposed with that of the detective who interviewed me about Bonnie's death, I decided to Google some articles about the police investigation. I found one that mentioned the lead investigator by his full name, Roger Frank Nielsen. Then I knew what I didn't want to believe, that he had to be the Frank that Bonnie was seeing…and may have murdered her because she rejected him or whatever."

Lance was flabbergasted at this possible development in the cold case. The notion that someone who was in the Honolulu Police Department could have been the unsub in Bonnie's death infuriated him to no end. If it were true that Nielsen was her killer, how did he get away with it? Did he have help covering up the crime? Could Lieutenant Powell have been involved or turned the other way in pursuing justice against one of their own?

"She's right," Caroline stated, looking at her cell phone. "Nielsen's middle name is Frank. This makes him a person of interest," she argued. "A little more than coincidence, I'd say."

"I mean, I could be way off base pointing the finger at him," Shelley allowed. "But as Bonnie's best friend, I felt I owed it to her—and you, Detective Warner—to bring this to you. Whatever happens from here, I'll know I did the right thing."

"You did," he agreed wholeheartedly. "And call me Lance." Somehow, talking with the professor whom Bonnie had entrusted, brought him back to when he was just a teenager and wanting more than anything to be able to hang out with his sister and her coed friends in Honolulu. He was never given that chance, but was at least able to make the acquaintance of one of them, after the fact.

"Mahalo," Shelley told him in a maudlin voice.

"Did you happen to ever mention to Nielsen that Bonnie was dating a man named Frank?" Lance wondered.

"Yes, I did. But at the time, since he was investigating the case and didn't flinch at hearing the name, I figured Frank must have been someone else." She paused. "If only I had spoken to one of the other investigators that he wasn't able to manipulate, maybe it would have made a difference."

Lance considered Powell and whether or not he was privy to this, which wasn't in the official case file. "Not necessarily," he told her candidly. "In fact, if Nielsen did kill Bonnie, not continuing to make waves about a lookalike man named Frank may well have saved your life."

Shelley's mouth hung open, aghast. "You think?"

"Quite possibly. If Nielsen viewed you as a threat to his secret identity, giving him a motive and opportunity for murder, he likely wouldn't have hesitated to go after you too."

As she contemplated that frightening prospect, Caroline asked, "Has Nielsen or anyone come around asking you questions or threatening you? Or otherwise making you feel as though you were being watched?"

"No, not that I can recall." Shelley cringed. "Should I be worried?"

Caroline hedged in glancing at Lance, then told her candidly, "There's something I think you need to know. We have good reason to believe that I was the intended target of the shooter at the substance abuse treatment center yesterday."

Shelley reacted. "Really?"

"The victim, Kirsten Vanderham, lived in the same apartment building as Bonnie at the time of her death. We were questioning her to this effect when the shots rang out." Caroline took a breath. "Anyway, my point is that we think someone, possibly Roger Nielsen, wants to keep the case closed as far as learning more about the murder..."

"Meaning you or anyone else the perpetrator views as a threat to exposure could be in danger," Lance finished. He didn't wish to frighten her to death. But considering the alternative, they needed to lay the cards out on the table for Bonnie's best friend, so she wasn't caught off guard by the unsub.

"So do I need to go into hiding, or what?" Shelley's voice shook. "Never mind the fact that I'm needed right now as a professor and have other obligations as well. But if my life is in jeopardy—"

"You don't necessarily need to disrupt your life entirely at this point," Caroline advised her gingerly. "If you haven't run into trouble yet, chances are the killer—whether it's Nielsen or another person—may not have you in his or her crosshairs. But just to be on the safe side, it's probably a good idea for the time being to be on your guard on campus and maybe stay with someone for a few days if you live alone."

"Will do," she promised, nervously adjusting her glasses.

"In the meantime, we'll certainly look into Roger Nielsen," Caroline assured her.

Lance seconded this, finishing off his drink. "Thanks for telling us this."

Shelley nodded. "If he did kill Bonnie, Frank deserves to be held accountable."

"If he killed my sister, believe me, Nielsen will be."

Chapter Eleven

Caroline could hardly believe that retired detective Roger Nielsen could have killed Bonnie and successfully covered his tracks for two decades. On the other hand, wasn't that the very essence of a cold case, one that went unsolved long enough that it was removed from ongoing investigations? Who was to say that Roger or Frank hadn't cleverly corrupted evidence and did whatever else was necessary to eliminate himself as a suspect? And did Lance's boss, Lieutenant Powell, help Nielsen cover his tracks? Caroline found herself skeptical at best with that theory, considering that her own boss had put her on the investigation into Bonnie's death at Powell's request.

Still, some things weren't adding up, Caroline knew. Could Shelley's belief that Bonnie's married lover was a police detective investigating her murder be a case of mistaken identity? Or could this shocking accusation be the smoking gun they were looking for? Caroline pondered this as she drove over to the hospital to check on Kirsten Vanderham, who had a guard stationed outside her door. All the while, Caroline had been ever vigilant in making sure she wasn't being followed, mindful of that old saying, *if at first you don't succeed...* She believed the unsub might well try again and she needed to be ready. Apart from being armed with her official weapon and quick on her feet, Caroline had learned Kapu Ku'ialua or Lua—an ancient Hawaiian martial art for self-defense—from her father. Though she'd never had to use it before, she wouldn't hesitate to defend herself in any way necessary against an assailant.

After leaving the hospital, Caroline headed over to the PD to meet up with Lance and Eliza. It was incumbent upon them to sort out fact from fiction. Or, in this instance, a detective who presumably retired in good standing with the police department, from one who was either a onetime killer or serial killer. Or neither. If nothing else, it allowed Caroline to sidetrack for now her renewed involvement with Lance and whether she could truly trust him to be there through thick and thin, and refocus her energies into solving the ligature murder of his sister.

"Detective Roger Nielsen was the first investigator at the scene of Bonnie's murder," Eliza said at her desk. This confirmed what Caroline had already discovered from the case file.

"So that gave him time to tamper with the evidence," Lance surmised, "including the murder weapon, which, if true, Nielsen may well have been wearing before and after the homicide took place."

Eliza wrinkled her brow. "You really believe that Nielsen could be your sister's killer?"

Lance's face hardened. "Why not? His full name is Roger Frank Nielsen. According to Bonnie's best friend, Shelley Pacheco, Bonnie was dating off and on a married man named Frank, whom Shelley met and believes that this Frank and Nielsen are one and the same. She claimed that Bonnie tried to break things off and Frank didn't want to let her go. Or possibly ruin his image at the time as a faithfully married man to Nielsen's first wife and a police detective. So, you tell me, who better to kill her to keep her from leaving him on the one hand or ruining his life on the other, than the very detective investigating the crime who was in a good position to manipulate the crime scene and destroy or remove evidence?"

"Point taken," Eliza said, averting his gaze. "Nielsen has to be considered a suspect all things considered."

"Which is why we need to learn everything about him during that time, right up to his retirement, and even what he may have been up to lately," Caroline put forth. "Where there's smoke, there's most likely fire, if not a full-blown inferno covering two decades. For instance, were there any complaints filed against Nielsen during that period and, if so, what became of them and any disciplinary actions?"

"I'll see what I can find out," Eliza told them. "But your best bet for a more complete picture of Nielsen's history and any trouble spots would be to talk to Lieutenant Powell, whose position in the cold case runs deep, along with his role in the current serial killer investigation."

"I'm way ahead of you there," Lance said firmly. "Normally, I'd want to make sure we had our ducks lined up before going to see the lieutenant. But some things can't wait. This is one of them."

"I'm on board with you there," Caroline told him, as it was obvious that they needed much more from Lieutenant Powell than they had gotten thus far, assuming he wasn't complicit himself in the murder of Bonnie Warner.

WHEN THEY WALKED into Powell's office, he was seemingly deep in thought at his desk. Or at least Lance sensed that he was weighed down by the demands of heading the Criminal Investigation Division of the Honolulu Police Department. Or perhaps he was sulking over a recent divorce that he claimed to have never seen coming till the papers were served. For his part, Lance was more interested in what Powell knew about Nielsen and when, while giving the lieutenant, whom he respected as a man of integrity, the benefit of the doubt that he hadn't been a party to covering for a killer for the past twenty years.

"Hey," Powell said, shifting his eyes at them. "What's up?"

"There's been a development," Lance responded vaguely.

"Oh…?" He flashed a curious look. "Go on…"

"It's about retired detective Roger Frank Nielsen," Caroline said.

Lance narrowed his eyes. "We have reason to believe Nielsen may be a person of interest in the death of my sister." Was it his imagination, or did the lieutenant not seem at all surprised?

Powell took a breath and ordered, "Close the door!" Afterwards, he asked them to sit down, before saying, "Tell me why you suspect Nielsen of having something to do with the murder?"

Lance deferred to Caroline as, technically speaking, this was her cold case and he was along for the ride but just as driven to see a resolution. "A witness has emerged that can link Detective Nielsen to Bonnie, beyond being the lead investigator into her death," she said intently. "He had apparently been romantically involved with Bonnie, sir."

"Really?" Powell looked uncomfortable. "And who is this witness?"

"Shelley Pacheco, Bonnie's best friend at the time, and now a professor at the University of Hawai'i at Mānoa." Caroline paused before continuing, "According to Shelley, Bonnie was seeing a married man named Frank. Only recently did Shelley come to realize that this Frank, whom she'd met, was in fact Roger Nielsen, who used his middle name to get Bonnie into bed, and maybe other young women as well. As a detective, Nielsen interviewed Shelley regarding Bonnie's murder and the name Frank was brought up, but the professor was unable to connect the dots till now."

"There was nothing from Nielsen's report in the case file that mentioned the name Frank as someone Bonnie had been seeing, and therefore would have become a suspect in her death," Lance pointed out. "Or, in other words, Nielsen, who was the first investigator at the crime scene, clearly covered up his involvement with the victim. Why? I'm guessing he had a damned good reason to hide this key fact, knowing he didn't have an alibi for the time of my sister's death, which would have made him a prime suspect." Lance's chin jutted. "Tell me you knew nothing about any of this, lieutenant," he challenged him.

"I didn't." Powell jerked his head. "Not in so many words…"

"What does that mean?" Lance demanded.

"Truthfully, it means that I had my suspicions about Nielsen from the start, but I could never prove anything. I certainly didn't know that he'd been romantically involved with the victim, though I knew he was prone to straying from his marriage from time to time. The idea that he may have been involved in

Bonnie's death did cross my mind but, again, there was nothing there to substantiate making such an accusation regarding a fellow officer of the law."

"Wasn't there anything in his personnel file that raised a red flag?" Caroline asked dubiously. "Surely there must have been complaints of unwanted attention or other areas of concern."

"That's the thing, there was nothing in his file to arouse suspicion," Powell insisted. "As far as any administrative or criminal complaints with the HPD's Professional Standards Office, Nielsen is clean." The lieutenant ran a hand across his bald head. "That being said, I've been uneasy about the ex-detective and what he might have been capable of for a long time. But then he went into early retirement and the case went cold. When a new homicide that had all the earmarks of Bonnie's murder occurred, it struck me as the right time to reopen the case and see if they were connected in any way. Or, at the very least, provide an opportunity to reinvestigate an old murder through a new lens for hopefully a different result." He met Lance's face with a steady gaze. "If your instincts about Roger Nielsen prove to have legs, then I'd say we may finally come one step closer to finding out once and for all who killed your sister."

"That's my thinking," Lance concurred thoughtfully. He was relieved that Powell seemed above board and not a party to Nielsen as a possible murderer and their two decades old unsub. But suspicions alone, short of solid evidence, would not be enough to bring down the retired detective. They needed more than Nielsen dating Bonnie behind his wife's back to charge him with murder. Maybe they could bring him in, shake him up a bit and get him to confess to what he'd done. Could that extend beyond Bonnie to the current victims of ligature strangulation?

"I think it's past time to bring Nielsen in for a little informal chat," Powell said, reading Lance's mind. "Let's hear what he has to say about this and take things from there. But before we open that possible can of worms, I think you should go see his ex-wife, Joan. She still lives on the island. Me and my own ex used to hang out with them. I run into her from time to time even now. Maybe she can give you some added insight into Nielsen and what he may have been up to at that time that could be useful when we get him in here."

Caroline glanced at Lance and said, "Good idea to talk with her. She could provide clues into his mindset and what he might have been capable of."

"We'll interview Nielsen's ex," Lance agreed. "Whatever it takes to help nail him, if he is indeed the unsub in Bonnie's death."

"And if you're off base, it will at least eliminate Nielsen as a suspect in one crime," Powell said, "while continuing to pursue any and all leads in another."

Lance didn't argue the point, knowing that the cold case was only half of what he was dealing with. The other half wasn't going away on its own. Not without his help. But at the moment, he needed to do right by his sister. He sensed that this latest twist had put them on a course toward solving the decades old mystery.

"WHY WOULD BONNIE get involved with someone like Nielsen, who was much older?" Lance grumbled while driving.

"It's not that difficult to imagine why," Caroline responded from the passenger seat of his vehicle, realizing he was venting more because of how her life ended than her dating habits beforehand. "A single college coed being turned off by guys her own age who are too caught up in themselves would find someone older, more established and wiser, appealing. Especially if he poured on the charm and made her feel special."

"Sounds like the voice of experience," he said, eyeing her inquisitively.

If Caroline hadn't known better, she would think that Lance was actually jealous of her love life before him. "Not exactly," she made clear. "I was never attracted to much older guys, not feeling that experience was necessarily the best teacher in my dating life. But I did know other starry-eyed coeds who would happily throw themselves into ill-fated relationships with college professors or others in their thirties or forties who put the moves on them, bought expensive gifts or whatever. I'm sure Bonnie saw something in Nielsen that appealed to her and she let it happen. But she was also smart enough, once she found out he was married, to cut him loose."

"I know," Lance conceded. "I'm proud of her for that. Only it may have come at a high price, assuming Nielsen really refused to take no for an answer and made sure no one else would ever have her."

"That's what we need to find out," Caroline uttered. She hoped the retired detective's ex-wife might shed just enough light on the man to tell them whether or not they were onto something. Or going on a wild goose chase, while Bonnie's real killer was someone else, possibly still at it.

They drove down Ala Moana Boulevard and pulled into the structure lot of the Ala Moana Center, billed as the largest open-air shopping mall in the world, and headed inside to the department store where Joan Nielsen worked in the beauty section. They found her behind the counter, wearing a name tag. A slender woman in her late fifties, she had brunette-gray hair worn in a graduated and feathered bob and blue eyes behind horn-rimmed glasses.

When she homed in on them, Caroline flashed her ID and said, "Detective Yashima, cold case investigator for the Attorney General's Criminal Justice

Division. This is Detective Sergeant Warner, Honolulu PD. Wonder if we could have a word with you?"

"Sure." Joan rested her hands on the glass counter. "To what do I owe this visit?" she asked guardedly.

"It's about your ex-husband, Roger Nielsen," Lance responded with an edge to his voice.

"I see." Caroline saw her expression change into one of despair. "I thought he was out of my life for good," Joan muttered. "Guess being married to a cop who never truly appreciated me till it was too late was bound to rear its ugly head again someday. What would you like to know?"

"We're looking into the death of Bonnie Warner, who was murdered twenty years ago," Caroline said, "while a graduate student at the University of Hawai'i at Mānoa."

"I remember the case," she said surely. "It was all the talk on the island at the time, with the killer on the loose."

Caroline glanced at Lance and back. "Bonnie was involved with a married man at the time named Frank. We have reason to believe that this man was Roger Nielsen, going by his middle name."

Joan didn't flinch. "I have no reason to dispute that. Roger was unfaithful throughout our marriage, in spite of my efforts to the contrary, and often used his middle name with family and friends," she acknowledged. "Frank was his father's name and Roger practically worshipped him when he was alive." Joan eyed Lance curiously. "Are you and Bonnie Warner related?"

"She was my sister," he said sullenly. "Nielsen was the lead detective in the murder investigation."

"Sorry for your loss," Joan said. "I know this was Roger's case. It was like his first big homicide investigation and he brought it home with him."

"What do you mean?" Caroline looked at her, seeking more clues toward zeroing in on Nielsen as a killer. Were their signs to preface a deviant pattern of behavior?"

"He was moody, as I recall, agitated, distant and just off his game somewhat. I figured it was just the pressure of trying to solve the murder."

"Nielsen claimed to us earlier that his dogged effort to crack the case is what led to your divorce," Lance said skeptically. "Is that true?"

"Not exactly," she contended. "I divorced Roger because I just couldn't take the cheating and lies any longer. I knew I was better off on my own. Have been ever since."

"Guess Nielsen saw things differently," Caroline pointed out, "In any event, he's now remarried to someone else and, by all accounts, seems to be living the good life in his retirement." *Or at least putting up a good front,* she mused, while wondering just how much of a façade it might be.

Joan winced. "If he and his current wife are happy, so be it. I'm so over Roger, trust me. After he got injured on the job and had to quit, we both knew that sympathy would not fix what was broken in the marriage, so we ended it."

"We wonder if what was broken in your ex went well beyond infidelity and occupational injury and leaving the force as a result," Caroline said, giving that a moment to settle.

Joan looked disconcertingly from her to Lance and back. "So, what exactly are you looking for?" she demanded.

"Nielsen never bothered to put in his report that he was involved with Bonnie," Lance said. "According to her best friend, once she realized he was married, Bonnie tried to break it off. Only Nielsen wouldn't leave her alone."

Caroline put forth bluntly, "We think your ex may have strangled Bonnie to death in a crime of passion, such as a fit of jealous rage, or to silence her to keep you in the dark about his extramarital activities."

Joan seemed genuinely taken aback at the idea that the man she was married to could be capable of cold-blooded murder. "I knew Roger was a louse as a husband and capable of going to extremes to get what—and who—he wanted, apparently including Bonnie. But committing murder…"

Lance's brow furrowed. "As a police detective myself, I wish I could believe that a former detective wouldn't stoop so low as the crime of murder. But the signs are pointing in that direction. My sister's been dead for more than two decades while her killer has gone unpunished. Nielsen had the motive and opportunity to perpetrate the crime and get away with it. If you know anything at all that can help us to solve this case, you need to speak up."

While she mulled that over, Caroline added what needed to be said, "Whether it's Roger Nielsen or a copycat killer, someone is currently killing young women the same way Bonnie was murdered. If that someone is Nielsen, he needs to be stopped. If it's someone else in his orbit, that person needs to be held accountable. Or else more women are going to die."

"Roger and I have been divorced for a long time," Joan stated reflectively. "We haven't kept in touch. I hope he hasn't gotten mixed up in any of these murders, especially the one from two decades ago." She sighed. "I don't know if this can be of any help or not... When we were still married, Roger kept some things in a storage unit. He never told me what—just that it was stuff he wanted to keep. I have no idea if he still has it or not or what might be inside. You'll have to ask him."

Exchanging glances with Lance, Caroline imagined they might do just that. Provided they were able to get a sit down with the former detective, who might also be a murderer hiding in plain view for years. But could he have also been a spouse abuser, past and present, as an indicator of Nielsen's proclivity for violent behavior? She regarded his ex and said probingly, "I need to ask, did Nielsen ever hit you or show any other aggressive behavior during your marriage, such as attempting to strangle you?"

Joan sucked in a deep breath before responding, a break in her voice, "We fought from time to time like other married couples. If Roger did cross the line, I let him know and he apologized. He never tried to strangle me." She paused. "Whether or not he did anything like that to other women he got involved with who didn't want to play by his rules, I couldn't say."

"Couldn't or won't?" Lance kept up the heat.

"I've told you everything I know," she maintained, her head lowered.

In Caroline's mind, Nielsen's ex had said a lot about the psyche of the man and his capabilities. She feared that infidelity and domestic violence could well have escalated into unstable and homicidal behavior, with Bonnie having the misfortune of getting caught up in his orbit.

Chapter Twelve

In the interrogation room, Lance and Caroline sat at the table across from Roger Nielsen. Lieutenant Powell stood nearby, insisting on being present during the interview of his former colleague. They had requested Nielsen's appearance under the guise of being an adviser in the cold case investigation. In fact, he was now seen as a prime suspect in the murder of Bonnie Warner. But given the voluntary and informal nature of the meeting, he didn't need to be advised of his right to an attorney at this time. Lance wondered how long it would take for that to change.

"Nice to see you again, Roger," Powell told him in a friendly voice. "Thanks for coming in."

"No problem," Nielsen said coolly. "Happy to help any way I can."

"Good, that's what we're counting on."

Powell glanced at Caroline with a nod to proceed. "Detective Nielsen," she began evenly, "in the course of our investigation into the death of Bonnie Warner, we discovered that sometime prior to her death

she was involved with a married man named Frank."
Caroline paused and glimpsed at the contents of a
file folder. "I don't see any mention of this Frank in
your report. Care to explain…?"

Nielsen swallowed. "Yes, I was aware of that," he
admitted shakily. "But at the time, it didn't seem relevant in the investigation to make note of."

"How could it not have been?" Lance challenged
him, peering at the man. "Especially when this man
might have been a prime suspect in the murder, given
their relationship."

"I was told that this Frank and the victim were no
longer seeing each other at the time of her death," he
claimed, "so he wasn't considered a suspect in the
investigation."

Powell faced him. "Roger, we know your full name
is Roger Frank Nielsen. We also know that you were
the one having an affair with Ms. Warner. Isn't that
true?"

Nielsen expressed fake outrage. "No, you're mistaken," he insisted. "Yeah, Frank is my middle name,
but that's about as close as—"

"Cut the crap, Nielsen." Caroline's voice hardened.
"We have an eyewitness who has identified you as
Frank, the married man whom Bonnie was seeing
and tried to end the relationship. Did you kill her for
revenge? Or to keep your dirty little secret from your
then-wife, Joan?"

Nielsen's jaws sagged. "All right, all right. I did

have a short affair with Bonnie. But I didn't kill her, I swear. We both decided to end the relationship once she found out I was married. I didn't want to lead her astray that we had a future, so I left her alone and we went our separate ways. When I learned she had been killed, I panicked, okay? I figured that if I came clean about the affair, it would make me a suspect, unjustly, and distract from finding the real killer. So I kept that information to myself."

"But you didn't find the killer, did you?" Lance hit him with a glower. "It's been twenty years and the case hasn't been solved. Why is that?" he demanded, trying hard to keep his temper in check. "Why isn't my sister's killer behind bars? Is it because I'm looking at him?"

"No, it's because the trail went ice cold," Nielsen replied audaciously, "in spite of my best efforts. I worked night and day to solve the case, knowing I owed her that much. It was just not to be. It happens that way sometimes."

"Not this time, Roger," Powell snapped, glaring at him. "We think you murdered that woman, using a leather belt like the type you used to wear, and tried to cover it up by hiding the evidence and omitting any mention of your involvement with her in the official record. Whether you planned it in advance as a retaliatory murder or it happened in the spur of the moment, I believe you forgot which side of the law you were supposed to be on and let your emotions get the better of you. As someone who once worked alongside you and considered you a friend, my advice is to fess up and get this off your chest in doing right by Bonnie Warner and the brother she left behind, Detective Sergeant Lance Warner."

Nielsen clammed up for a long moment, as if weighing his options. Finally, he said defiantly, "Do I need a lawyer?"

"That's entirely up to you," Caroline told him curtly. "But once you go down that road, all bets are off. Including the fact that someone took a shot at me, hitting Kirsten Vanderham instead. That makes it attempted murder, along with the murder of Bonnie Warner. If you're also behind the similar ligature strangulation murders of Jill Hussey and Sophie O'Rourke, you've got even more trouble to deal with. Need I go on…?"

"Look, I never tried to kill you," Nielsen blared, "and I sure as hell had nothing to do with those other murders."

"Mind telling us what type of firearm you own?" she asked dubiously.

"I keep a Smith & Wesson M&P 10mm pistol for self-protection," he answered matter-of-factly.

Lance considered that the shooter at the substance abuse treatment center used a 9mm Luger pistol. It wasn't out of the question that Nielsen could own more than one firearm. "That hardly lets you off the hook," he warned him. "All three women were strangled to death and the killer or killers took one of the victims' shoes as a memento of the kill. This makes you still the number one suspect in my book." *At least for Bonnie's murder*, Lance thought, with the jury still out for the other homicides.

Nielsen remained unaffected. "None of this makes any sense." He eyed Powell pleadingly. "Dorian, we go back a long way. How could you even think I'd be capable of killing someone I actually cared about? Or actually went after Detective Yashima and, what, have now suddenly become a serial killer?"

"Maybe it's not so sudden, Roger," Powell retorted. "Maybe this was twenty years in the making, starting with a college coed who you crossed the line with, then murdered to keep her from spilling the beans, even if Joan was also privy to your being unfaithful to her. And lastly, you wanted to cover this up to protect your career and remain a free man. So, what's it going to be, Roger, do you want representation?"

Before he could answer, Lance announced boldly, "You're free to go, Nielsen. We obviously don't have enough to hold you. Much less charge with anything. Maybe we should be looking elsewhere."

Nielsen cracked a relieved grin as he rose. "Glad that at least you have come to your senses, Warner. I'm not your man from twenty years ago or now." He sneered at Powell and locked in on Caroline. "Good luck with solving Bonnie's murder," he said smugly.

"I want to see her killer apprehended as much as you do, believe it or not. And the recent murders solved as well…"

Using a cane, Roger Nielsen walked out of the interrogation room on that note and Lance waited a beat, before saying confidently, "He's as guilty as sin. I can feel it in my gut."

Caroline nodded. "I share those sentiments. At the very least, Nielsen is the person most likely responsible for Bonnie's death."

"I'm getting that sense too," Powell said. "But it was a smart move to allow him to believe otherwise by letting him walk at this point, with no hard evidence to tie Nielsen to any of the murders just yet."

Lance agreed, painful as it was to see the man he believed had strangled Bonnie to death, snubbing his nose at them while thinking he would successfully continue to circumvent the law. Short of a confession, which never came, releasing Nielsen to go about his business was their only real option for the time being. "We need to see if he still has the storage unit," Lance thought out loud, "and, if so, get a look inside it."

"We're looking into that." The lieutenant ran a hand across his bald head. "In the meantime, we have a man on Nielsen, watching where he goes and what he does. Maybe he'll lead us to evidence of his guilt. Or further intentions, deadly or not."

I'm not holding my breath that Nielsen will hand

us evidence of his guilt on a silver platter, Lance thought bleakly, as he got to his feet. But that didn't mean they weren't onto him as Bonnie's killer and willing to go after him in proving this, one way or the other.

Caroline stood and they waited till Powell had left the room, before Lance said, "We're closer than ever to giving Bonnie the peace she has long deserved."

"I agree." She offered him a nice smile, bringing back fresh memories of last night.

He smiled back. "So, am I ever going to get to see that Waikiki condo of yours?"

Caroline chuckled. "Didn't know you were that interested in seeing it," she teased him.

Lance's eyes twinkled. "I'm interested in anything and everything that involves you and your life," he made clear.

"Oh, really?"

"Do you doubt it?" He wavered thoughtfully. "Don't answer that."

"Good move." She laughed. "If you like, you can drop by the condo for a drink this evening, say eight?"

"I'd like," Lance said solidly. "Eight, it is." He was already looking forward to taking a small detour from the investigations and being in her territory for whatever happened to come their way.

THAT EARLY HUMID EVENING, Caroline walked barefoot on the soft sand of Fort Derussy Beach, along Waikiki's oceanfront. Beside her was Rachelle Compagno, her attorney friend and fellow resident at the condo high-rise across the street. Both had their water bottles and managed to separate themselves from other beachgoers. Happy to enjoy a little girl time before another get together later with Lance, Caroline listened as Rachelle talked about a new man she was dating. "His name is Harold Horikoshi," she said. "He's a fire dancer by night and, get this, a firefighter by day."

Caroline laughed. "That's so funny."

"Right?"

"He must have a few stories to tell about the risks and rewards of fire and all that," Caroline half joked, feeling the ponytail bounce against the back of her neck.

"Quite a few tales, both lighthearted and heartbreaking." Rachelle ran a hand down her French braid. "We're still just feeling each other out, but so far, so good."

"That's wonderful to hear." Caroline debated as to whether to reveal her renewed relationship with Lance. Or not.

Rachelle seemed to sense this as she said, "So, what's been happening between you and Detective Warner. Or shouldn't I ask?"

"You probably shouldn't." Caroline chuckled. "But I'll tell you anyhow. We've sort of started seeing each other again."

"Seriously?" Rachelle's eyes widened. "Uh, we are talking about over and beyond working a cold case, right?"

"Yes, over and beyond that." Caroline blushed as she thought about their red-hot night in bed. "Seems like I never truly got him out of my system," she admitted, in spite of her best efforts to the contrary when it appeared as though they were over and done with for good.

"And clearly that works both ways," Rachelle said playfully. "Now that Lance is back on your best side, maybe the four of us can get together soon. I'm sure that Harold and Lance would hit it off."

Caroline wasn't quite ready to say that she and Lance were a couple. Not to mention start thinking again in terms of a long-term future with the detective. Still, she liked the idea of them being together and hanging out with friends. So she told Rachelle, while making no definite plans just yet, "That sounds great."

"Cool." Rachelle took a breath. "Speaking of your partnering with Lance, have you two gotten any closer to identifying his sister's killer after so many years have passed by?"

"As a matter of fact, we have," Caroline told her, and considered the bead they had on former police detective Roger Nielsen. They had yet to prove their case, but he was definitely their prime suspect as Bonnie's assailant. Still, not wanting to get ahead of herself or jinx the investigation, Caroline said, "Unfortunately, I'm not at liberty to go into the details just yet, for fear of jeopardizing the case."

"Understood," Rachelle said, pivoting as they headed off the beach. "Can you at least tell me if that cold case is connected at all to the so-called Belt Strangler?"

"We're still looking into that," Caroline admitted. Was Nielsen the perp responsible for the latest ligature strangulations of women in Honolulu? Or a convenient scapegoat for someone else? "If I had to give you a yes or no," she told her friend, "I'd have to say that they probably are connected. At least on some level." And with that thought alone, Caroline felt unnerved, knowing they still had their work cut out for them in putting all the pieces together.

LANCE MARVELED AS he took in Caroline's impressive Waikiki condo that seemed to have everything a woman could want in a high-rise residence, including an amazing view of Diamond Head. Everything, that was, except for a man who could give her even more, if she would let him. But would she ever want to give up her prime location and move in with him? Or he could just as easily see himself living there, if it was what she wanted. Had his bad judgement call two and a half years ago come back to haunt him, now that he knew what he wanted beyond a career in law enforcement?

"Nice," Lance found himself saying, as he gave the place a sweeping look.

"Mahalo." Caroline's beautiful face lit with pride as she handed him a Honolulu #3 cocktail, which consisted of gin, lime juice, Benedictine, lavender bitters, and soda water. She looked relaxed in a cold-shoulder top and cuffed Bermuda shorts, her feet bare. "It's been a good fit for me," she said, sipping her own drink.

"I don't doubt that." He took a sip of the delicious cocktail. "You deserve everything you have in life."

"Thanks." She met his gaze. "So do you."

"Not sure I have everything I want." Lance felt that was an understatement. Especially being so near to the one thing he wanted most, having a full life with the woman before him.

Caroline's lashes batted daringly. "What else do you want?"

"The whole package," he said straightforwardly. Realizing that was insufficient in telling her what she wanted to hear, Lance stated in plain language, "I want you. All of you."

"Really?" she uttered sexily. "You can have me. As long as I get to have you back." She paused. "Beyond that, we'll see…"

Not wanting to risk the good thing they had going, Lance backed off asking for more, much more, just yet. Unlike before, he needed to do this right for it to work for both of them on a permanent basis. He only wished Caroline had gotten to know Bonnie. And vice versa. They could have bridged his past and present in a way that no one else could have. He would have to settle for Caroline doing her part to help him heal in losing his sister to an act of criminality; which would in its own way bind them together, transcending time.

In Caroline's bedroom, Lance saw white Montauk solid wood furnishings, including a platform bed. As she pulled down the microfiber duvet cover and began removing her clothes, he took off his Henley tee, jeans, and footwear, put on protection, and scooped Caroline into his arms. They went to bed and made love, setting aside the cases that brought them back together in favor of the romantic vibes and sexual compatibility engulfing them like a firestorm. After bringing each other the pleasure they needed and physical merging that came with it, Lance pulled Caroline against his body, delighting in the softness of her skin. He was still very much in love with her. Was she ready to hear this? Or would her resistance out of fear of having her heart broken act as a natural barrier?

After falling asleep, Lance awakened, as disturbing thoughts fell into his subconscious. Caroline was stirred awake. "What is it?" she asked intuitively.

He clenched his jaw. "I think he may have been there."

"Who? Where?"

"Roger Nielsen," Lance said glumly. "A couple of weeks before Bonnie's death, I called her. We talked a little about nothing in particular, but I remembered thinking that she sounded tense. When I asked her what was wrong, she said nothing, then told me, 'Wait, Lance.' Her voice was then muffled like she'd put her hand over the mouthpiece. I couldn't quite make out what she was saying and didn't give it much thought afterward." He shifted in the bed to face her more fully. "The more I think back, the more I believe that Bonnie said, 'Leave, Frank. It's over.'"

Caroline put her hand on his. "You really think that?"

"Yeah." Lance furrowed his brows. "I know it probably sounds crazy, but maybe this was Bonnie attempting to extricate herself from a doomed relationship before things got out of hand, but tried to do it all on her own."

"It doesn't sound crazy, Lance," Caroline insisted, surprising him. "Odd as it seems, maybe on some level, this is Bonnie reaching out from the grave to assist you and me in exposing her killer and bringing him to justice."

"You think?" he asked, even doubting himself.

"Yes, why not?" She rested her head on his shoulder. "Who's to say how the universe works? We both feel that Roger Nielsen is the culprit. Now it's up to us, with help from your sister, to prove it."

"We will," Lance said. Relaxing his features, he lifted Caroline's chin and kissed her affectionately on the lips. He took solace in her backing him on this and being equally committed to seeking justice for Bonnie's murder. Another reason for loving the cold case investigator and being just as determined to prove this to her, when all was said and done.

Chapter Thirteen

The body of the victim, twenty-seven-year-old Olivia Madekwe, was found in a home on Kilauea Avenue in Waialae Nui Valley, an upscale neighborhood in Honolulu. She had been strangled, by all accounts, and missing one of the shoes she was wearing. Lance was troubled by this latest murder that came to light the next morning, after spending the night with Caroline. It had the stark effect of shifting his focus back to the current spate of serial homicides occurring in the city and away from Bonnie's death and its disturbing undercurrents. Even so, he still believed that the two were interconnected in one way or another, with Roger Nielsen continuing to be the prime suspect in his sister's death, at the very least. Caroline felt the same, giving them a person of interest to home in on.

Weaving his way through a full-blown crime scene with officers and technicians at work to secure and protect evidence, Lance flashed his identification routinely, as he stepped past Foxtail palm trees and inside the two-story luxury residence and onto cork flooring. He was immediately met in the great room by Detective Gushiken, who said grimly, "It looks like the Belt Strangler may have struck again."

Lance frowned. "Who discovered the body and where?"

"The victim's live-in boyfriend, Akeem Elba, found her in a bedroom upstairs. According to Elba, when he got home at nine a.m. after working the night shift as a Hospital Service Technician, she was dead. He swears she was alive and well, watching television, when he left just before midnight."

"Hmm…" Lance muttered thoughtfully, while considering that this would have given someone else ample time to commit the crime. "Where is he now?"

"We have him in a squad car for now, while verifying his alibi," Gushiken said.

"Good. Let's have a look at the victim." Lance followed him up a straight staircase and into the master suite with contemporary furnishings. Lying atop a quilted comforter on a rattan bed was Olivia Madekwe. Dark-skinned, she was slender and had black hair with long curly blonde ombré sew-ins. She was fully clothed in multicolored loungewear and had on a single brown mule slipper. The discoloring around her neck was evidence that it was where she was victimized. "Assuming the boyfriend's story holds up, the perp had to have been lying in wait for the opportunity to attack her."

"Yeah," Gushiken agreed. "But as of now, there are no clear signs of breaking and entering, so I'm thinking that the victim either let her assailant in, or he managed to slip in somehow and kill her."

"Either way you slice it," Lance said candidly, "the serial killer doesn't seem to be letting up and is sticking with the MO." Which made things increasingly worrisome for him as Lance considered all angles.

The medical examiner arrived and they allowed him to do his work with the deceased, after which Dr. Espiritu attributed the cause of death to ligature strangulation in his preliminary assessment, while estimating the time of death to be somewhere between midnight and three o'clock.

"You still think this is tied to your sister's death, don't you?" Gushiken looked at Lance knowingly, as they left the house.

"Someone sure as hell wants us to believe the dots are connected." In Lance's mind, that person was Roger Nielsen. But could he pull this off and escape easily while walking or running with a cane? Or was the cane more for appearance's sake, belying his true capabilities for getting around? As far as Lance knew, the man was still being trailed and unable to be in two places at once. Could he have an accomplice in murder?

Gushiken added to this when he said, in reading into Lance's musings, "We ran a check and Nielsen does have a permit to own a Smith & Wesson M&P 10-mm- handgun."

"I suspected as much, given that he volunteered the information." Lance was hardly convinced, however, that the man hadn't been the perp to shoot at Caroline. "I question, though, whether this is his only firearm. Especially if Nielsen wanted to do some damage with an illegal gun to try and stop us from solving the decades old murder."

"That's true. Wouldn't put it past him, if he's got something to hide. Desperate people, even bad ex-cops who like to stay out of jail, do desperate and dangerous things."

"Just what I'm afraid of." Lance was concerned about this on dual levels, as they tried to close in on one or two diabolical killers, with the clock ticking.

"WE'VE LOCATED A storage facility that Roger Nielsen is using," Lance informed Caroline later that day in a video chat, as she sat in her office.

"Really?" she said, perking up, gazing at his face.

"Yeah. According to the officer following him, Nielsen brought something to the unit on Kalauo-kalani Way, but left empty-handed."

"Hmm…that's interesting." Caroline would give anything to see what he had stored in the storage unit. Perhaps something incriminating? "We need a search warrant to check it out." She was sure that, given the stakes and strong suspicions that Nielsen may have been hiding evidence of a twenty-year-old murder if not more recent homicides, Vera would be able to pull a few strings and make it happen as Administrator of the Attorney General's Criminal Justice Division.

"Already two steps ahead on that," Lance said with a sideways grin in reading her mind. "Once I took this to Powell, he made a call and got a judge to authorize the search of Nielsen's unit."

"That's great," she said, while tempering expectations. "If Nielsen is our unsub, hopefully he will have kept something to prove his guilt."

"Only one way to find out. I'll swing by and pick you up and we can check it out together."

"Can't wait." She smiled at him. "See you soon."

Twenty minutes later, they were en route to the destination. During the mostly quiet drive, Caroline thought about Lance's dream, memory, epiphany or whatever you wanted to call it, believing that he overheard Bonnie saying to Roger Nielsen, "*Leave, Frank. It's over.*" While definitely not superstitious, and Caroline did not put much stock in ghostly messages across time, she believed that maybe on some cosmic or spiritual level, this was a way for Lance to reconnect with his sister and find clues from the past to lead to a resolution to the crime in the present. At least Caroline was willing to give him the benefit of the doubt in accepting his truth as reality. Just maybe the storage unit would give them evidence they needed to pin Bonnie's murder on the former detective.

When Lance updated her on the death of Olivia Madekwe, the latest ligature strangulation murder linked to the Belt Strangler, Caroline flinched. This made three young women strangled to death and at least one killer still on the loose. "Do you think that Nielsen was behind it?" she asked, while realizing they had been watching him since his interrogation.

"Hard to say," Lance responded thoughtfully. "Seemed like it would have been hard for him to pull it off all by himself, considering the surveillance. But then again, as an ex-cop, Nielsen likely would be able to spot this a mile away and know how to give them the slip, if he wanted. Especially at night when the murder occurred."

Caroline didn't disagree, but kept an open mind as she said, "That's certainly possible. Or he could be working in conjunction with another killer in following his lead."

"The two cases could still be separate," Lance pointed out, "but bound together in some way we've yet to figure out."

"And it's driving me crazy," she had to admit. "Cold and current cases can make for perplexing bedfellows."

"Yeah. And I'm just as crazy as you, which makes us great detectives."

She chuckled. "I suppose." And also made them great to be around one another in their private lives, which Caroline was starting to embrace again.

They reached the storage facility and made their way to Nielsen's unit, where Caroline and Lance executed the search warrant, accompanied by detectives from both their departments. Entering the unit, they saw boxes stacked in a disorderly fashion and various loose items scattered about.

"Let's see what's in here," Lance ordered.

"Or not," Caroline put out realistically.

Donning nitrile gloves, the search began for anything that even remotely could be viewed as evidence of a crime or otherwise of a suspicious nature. After several minutes of opening boxes, bags, and folders, and finding only normal collectibles and junk to hold onto, and no smoking guns, Caroline began to wonder if Nielsen had been smart enough to cover his tracks. Assuming they needed to be covered. Then she pulled out a box buried beneath other boxes. It was labeled, Bonnie.

This caused Caroline's heart to skip a beat. "I think I've found something," she said.

Lance helped her carry the box to an open area and set it down, as he read his sister's name out loud. "Let's get it open."

Using a box cutter, Caroline sliced through strapping tape and they lifted the flaps. Inside she homed in on a plastic bag containing a single high-heeled thong sandal and a black double loop-stitched leather belt with a single prong buckle. She lifted it out of the box and gazed at Lance, ill at ease. "You thinking what I'm thinking?"

"Yeah, how could I not." His voice broke. "Looks like Bonnie's missing shoe. And the type of leather belt used to strangle her."

Caroline was of the same mind. "That bastard kept the trophies of his kill all these years, just as FBI Special Agent and profiler Matthew Eleneki had indicated Nielsen might."

"And, apparently, Nielsen didn't stop his killing ways with Bonnie," Lance said sullenly, as he turned back toward the box.

Following his gaze, Caroline spied several other plastic bags. Each contained shoes that fit the description of the missing ones of the Belt Strangler's victims. Including the latest victim, as Lance indicated; along with black leather belts.

HOURS LATER, Lance and Caroline were in the Forensic Biology Unit of the HPD's Scientific Investigation Section, where crime laboratory analyst Juliet Raju had analyzed the contents of the box for DNA or fingerprints.

"We've got a solid match on DNA taken from the thong sandal you brought in," Juliet announced. "It matches DNA from the other sandal that was worn by the victim, your sister, Bonnie Warner," she told Lance sorrowfully. "Or, in other words, Bonnie was wearing the sandal you found in the storage unit the day she died."

Lance sighed in confirming what he had already ascertained. Nielsen had murdered his sister, then took and held onto the shoe as a sick keepsake. "What about other DNA on the shoe?"

"It matches that found on the first shoe in evidence," Juliet replied. "We can again send it to the Federal DNA Database Unit to be analyzed for a hit with someone in the National DNA Index System, but you'll need to collect the suspect's DNA to confirm it's a match."

"And the leather belt?" Caroline asked her.

"We were able to pull DNA from it, which matches DNA found on the victim's sandal. Unfortunately, we couldn't retrieve any fingerprints from the belt. My guess is the suspect wiped it clean before bagging it."

Lance wasn't at all surprised, considering that Nielsen, as a former detective, would know how to, if not remove, at least corrupt any fingerprints from evidence. But that was from twenty years ago. Had he been as careful with the more recent evidence? "What about the shoes and belts found in the other bags in the storage unit?"

Juliet ran a hand across an eyebrow. "We've got nothing, thus far, on the leather belts," she said apologetically. "As for the shoes, each contained DNA and prints that belonged to the victims of the Belt Strangler. Matching with the crime scene evidence, it appears these are the missing shoes taken from Jill Hussey, Sophie O'Rourke, and the last victim, Olivia Madekwe."

Caroline bobbed her head. "Which would indicate that their killer—Roger Nielsen—took them after finishing off the victims, and added them to his original trophy shoe."

"So it would seem." Juliet looked at Caroline and then at Lance. "Again, we weren't able to pull any other workable DNA or prints off the shoes or belts, as yet. But as you can see, when you put it all together—the likely murder weapons and victims' belongings…"

"We've identified my sister's killer and a modern-day serial killer all in one," Lance said acrimoniously. "It's time for Nielsen to answer for his crimes." *I owe Bonnie that much*, he told himself. The other victims needed him to be held accountable too.

"He will," Caroline said determinedly. "There's nowhere for him to hide anymore."

"Nielsen's red Volkswagen Taos SUV was spotted on a surveillance camera near the Aloha Substance Abuse Treatment Center around the time the shots rang out," Powell told them in his office. "Meaning it's a good chance he was the unsub gunning for you that day, Caroline."

She blinked as it sank in that the ex-detective-turned-killer had wanted her dead in order to protect his secret of murdering Bonnie. To Caroline, this seemed more important to Roger Nielsen than being exposed as the Belt Strangler. As though one could be expected to be a natural progression of the other. The fact that he had somehow managed to outsmart authorities then and now only showed her just how cunning Nielsen had been.

"Guess I should be thankful that he was probably in too much of a hurry to get away to aim properly," she said, though wishing Kirsten Vanderham hadn't taken a bullet instead.

"Yeah, thank goodness for small favors," Lance said sarcastically. "We need to bring Nielsen in before he can do any more damage."

"Agreed." Powell narrowed his eyes. "I think he's enjoyed a free ride long enough."

"That we all can agree on," Caroline seconded.

An arrest warrant was issued for Roger Nielsen, who was labeled as armed and dangerous. Before it could be served, the murder suspect went on the run, managing to dodge authorities. Apparently, he knew they were onto him as the Belt Strangler who began his murderous ways with the ligature strangulation of Bonnie Warner, and was not willing to end this thing peacefully.

A BOLO was put out for the suspect and his VW

SUV, with Caroline hoping they could bring Nielsen in alive to not only answer for his crimes with a life-time behind bars, but to also fill in the blanks on the past two decades and whether or not there were any other victims who may still be missing or labeled as cold cases. When the call came in that the suspect's vehicle had been spotted parked in a lot on Lagoon Drive, not far from the Daniel K. Inouye International Airport, Caroline relayed this to Lance as he drove.

"We're just a couple of minutes away," he said, increasing his speed. "It's even more painful when one of our own takes the deadly path Nielsen chose."

"True," she concurred. "Happens, though. Especially when someone like Nielsen decides he's above the law he was sworn to serve when not in his own best interests."

"Killing my sister should not have been something he decided to undertake." Lance made a groaning sound. "I want to ask him face-to-face why the hell couldn't he have left her alone and found someone else to be unfaithful with."

"Good luck in getting some answers," Caroline said doubtfully. "Cheating men like Nielsen often want to call the shots in their illicit affairs and can't seem to take rejection. But it certainly takes a spe-cial obsessive type to carry this over into murder-ing the lover, ex-lover, or whatever. And when and why he took this to another homicidal level as a serial killer is another twist that needs resolution—if we can get it."

"We'll take one thing at a time in seeking justice." Lance drove across the parking lot. "There's his car." It was parked away from other vehicles, with police cars keeping their distance as well.

Exiting their own vehicle, Caroline and Lance were both wearing Level IV body armor as they met up with Hugo Gushiken. "What's he doing?" Caroline asked.

"Just sitting there," Gushiken said. "Been that way since I arrived."

"Has anyone tried talking to him?" Lance asked.

"Yeah," the detective said. "No response. Probably just weighing his options now that he's cornered."

"Maybe he's already done that and decided they weren't very good," Caroline said, getting a bad feeling about the suspect.

"We need to end this one way or the other," Lance declared, removing his duty weapon. She did the same. "Let's move in," he ordered.

As law enforcement converged on the car, with Caroline as prepared to shoot as take return fire, she saw that the suspect was sitting motionless in his car on the driver's side. Upon closer inspection, it became clear that he had sustained a gunshot wound to the head. She spotted the firearm that had fallen onto his lap. Rather than turn himself in for the terrible things he'd done, Roger Nielsen had chosen to take his own life.

Chapter Fourteen

According to the medical examiner, Roger Nielsen
died from a single gunshot wound to the head. It
was ruled a suicide. Ballistics supported this finding, determining that the weapon used, a Smith &
Wesson CSX 9mm Luger pistol, had Nielsen's fingerprints all over it, and that the bullet removed from
his brain matched the ballistic markings on the spent
shell casing as well as the gun barrel's five lands and
grooves with a right-hand twist. Moreover, the bullet matched those fired at Caroline at the substance
abuse treatment center, indicating that they came
from the same weapon and shooter.

Lance was disappointed, but not at all surprised
that Nielsen had tried to silence Caroline, and when
that failed, ultimately found himself backed into
a proverbial corner and saw no way out. He left a
handwritten note confessing to the murder of Bonnie
Warner, whom he called his soulmate in another life.
Nielsen admitted to keeping the evidence to remind

him of her. He apologized to his second wife Dorothy, claiming he couldn't go to prison and wanted to
spare her from any further pain by ending his time
on Earth. There was no mention of the other homicide victims of ligature strangulation.

This didn't set well with Lance. Though the evidence strongly supported Nielsen being the so-called
Belt Strangler, why not confess to it in a life-ending
declaration to the family members of his victims?
If not law enforcement, whom he was once a member of.

"Maybe this was just his way of still having some
semblance of control over the final narrative," Caroline suggested as they left the Scientific Investigation Section the day after Nielsen's suicide. "Could
be he saw no benefit in clearing his conscience of
the added murders, as apparently only the killing
of Bonnie had an impact on his psyche and moving
forward thereafter. Besides, we have the evidence
tying him to the ligature murders."

"You're probably right," Lance said, regarding
the way Nielsen chose to leave things on his way
out. "And, yes, we did find the missing shoes and
belts used to strangle the women in his storage unit.
I guess some things are meant to be left hanging
to some degree." He wondered if that was a meta-
phor for their relationship. There was no question
in Lance's mind as to where he stood. He wanted
to spend the rest of his life with Caroline. But how

could he convince her of his sincerity and be believed?

She seemed to pick up on that and said, "And other things have a way of working themselves out when the dust settles."

Lance took that as a positive sign for them. "I can accept that."

They dropped by Lieutenant Powell's office to brief him on the dual cases. He wrinkled his brow and said, "I'm still trying to wrap my head around the idea that Nielsen, who I worked with, had stooped so low in carrying out these homicides over the past two decades. I keep asking myself if I could or should have done anything differently after he killed Bonnie to uncover the truth long before he could go after other young women."

"I doubt it." Feeling for the lieutenant, Lance cut him some slack. "We all second guess things in life, believe me." He gazed at Caroline and she smiled thinly, which Lance interpreted as her understanding his position. "In this case, Nielsen managed to dupe everyone. Including his two wives. As well as my sister. By the time she could see right through him as someone she wanted no part of, it was too late to save herself."

"Hopefully, she can rest in peace now," Powell said from behind his desk.

"My sentiments exactly." Lance only wished he could somehow tell her that in person. He would have to settle for the solace that Bonnie would no longer be restless in her grave, knowing her killer was still at large all these years later.

"Same goes for the other women who had the misfortune of falling victim to the likes of Roger Nielsen," Caroline reminded them.

Powell nodded. "Absolutely."

Lance felt for the other victims too. "They all deserve some sort of spiritual closure for lives that ended so tragically and way before their time," he said maudlinly.

"And you two deserve props for solving these cases for all the victims."

"Just doing our job," Caroline said modestly.

"Yeah." Lance agreed, even if he knew it went much further than that. But he didn't need to convince either of them of that, all things considered.

"Now get out of my office," Powell barked. "I'm sure you both have other stuff going on."

Lance grinned, knowing there were more cases that commanded his attention. He was sure the same was true with Caroline as well. Not to mention where they went from here on a personal level still needed to be worked out.

CAROLINE AND LANCE met with Shelley Pacheco in the courtyard garden at UH Mānoa to thank her for her role in identifying Bonnie's killer and closing the case. to Caroline, it was the least they could do after

Shelley's fortunate reawakening of lost memories. "Mahalo for helping us to expose Roger Nielsen as a murderer," she told Bonnie's best friend.

Lance followed up on that, as they stood among Hawaiian flowering plants. "My sister can finally have the peace she deserves."

"I'm glad this is finally over," Shelley expressed, teary-eyed. "Bonnie was my best friend. She'll always be a part of me, wherever I go. Just as I know the same holds true for you, Lance."

"Yes, always," he said somberly.

Shelley regarded them. "Would it be all right if I gave a Hawaiian traditional prayer for Bonnie's spirit?"

Lance grinned. "By all means."

"Please do," Caroline agreed, in honoring the heritage and customs of the Islands where she was born.

When Shelley was done, they promised to keep in touch with her. Caroline felt as though she and Lance had turned a page in their relationship, with solving Bonnie's death a big part of it. The one question left was whether or not Lance's feelings for her were as strong as hers for him and, if so, what he planned to do about it.

Neither tackled the issue squarely as Caroline went back to work, as did Lance, with plans to meet for dinner and talk about their future. If it was up in the air, she needed to know and proceed from there, even if any thoughts Caroline had of not having a life with Lance depressed her. But was he ready to make that kind of commitment if given another chance to do so, now that a big impediment to it had been lifted?

In her office, Caroline had a video chat on her laptop with Eliza about the closing of the cold case.

"I still hate to think that someone in our ranks, or used to be, turned to homicidal behavior, first with Bonnie Warner and then those other poor women," Eliza bemoaned.

"Right?" Caroline frowned. "You just never know. Roger Nielsen was obsessed with Bonnie and took it way too far," she said, which was an understatement. "Who knows why he came out of killer retirement, cane and all, to resume his killing ways. Or if Nielsen made a connection with any of the victims that went sour, causing him to lash out."

Eliza tilted her face. "Guess he took that mystery with him to the grave."

"Dead and buried." Caroline was inclined to agree, even if sensing there could be more to the story yet to unfold.

"Listen, if you ever get tired of working for the Attorney General's Criminal Justice Division, we'd love to have you with our Cold Case Unit," Eliza declared.

Caroline laughed. "I'll keep that in mind. Same holds true with you in reverse. We can always use another smart and capable detective in the CJD."

"Maybe I'll take you up on that someday," she said.

After disconnecting, Caroline imagined working for the HPD, with both Eliza and Lance. Or she could also see them as investigators with her department. Either way she looked at it, Caroline suspected the teamwork would be there. As it was, she was happy to be able to make her own contribution to the cause, be it solving old cases or putting the brakes on new ones.

Half an hour later, she was standing in Vera Miyasato's spacious office with new ergonomic furnishings and a picture window, where Caroline received the expected praise for completing her latest cold case assignment and accepted it graciously. "We're issuing a press release on the case this afternoon," Vera informed her. "I've sent it to you to look over and fill in anything you think is necessary to summarize the case against Roger Nielsen and his ultimate downfall after twenty years on the lam."

"Will do." Caroline smiled faintly. She understood that this came with the territory and, as such, didn't complain, even if she preferred to simply do her job and leave the writing about it to others at the CJD.

They talked for a minute or two about other current cold cases and new ones awaiting, before Caroline headed back to her office.

LANCE WENT TO the Scientific Investigation Section for routine follow up on the Belt Strangler investigation, before putting it to rest. Along with the serial killer, Roger Nielsen. Afterward, Lance planned to lay his heart on the line to Caroline and see if it was enough for her to take a chance again on them as a couple that he hoped would turn into becoming husband and wife.

When he approached Juliet Raju, Lance saw her face light up. "There's been a new development," she said keenly.

"Okay…" He waited for her to continue.

"Turns out that Olivia Madekwe, the last victim of the Belt Strangler, was able to get some of the killer's DNA under her fingernails."

"Really?" Lance's brows knitted. He was glad that she had fought back against Nielsen, even if she lost the battle.

"We ran it through CODIS to see if there was a match," Juliet told him. "We got a hit. Turned out to be a candidate match found in the Arrestee and Convicted Offender Indices." She paused. "It belonged to Kurt Preston."

"Kurt Preston…?" Lance considered the name, remembering him as the ex-boyfriend of Jill Hussey and suspect in her murder. He'd had an alibi for his whereabouts.

"Yes. Preston has been arrested for a DUI and drug possession. He also served time for assault and battery." Juliet wrinkled her nose. "There's more… We were able to pull a partial print from the plaque buckle of the leather belt we believe was used to strangle to death Sophie O'Rourke. It was sent to the Hawaii Criminal Justice Data Center and entered into the Automated Fingerprint Identification System. Another hit," she exclaimed. "The print also belonged to Kurt Preston. Looks as though for at least two of the homicides attributed to a modern-day serial killer, it was Preston and not Roger Nielsen who murdered both O'Rourke and Madekwe," the criminalist asserted.

"Which makes Preston a prime suspect in the killing of his former girlfriend, Jill Hussey," Lance deduced, assessing the bombshell forensic evidence that supported the Belt Strangler as being Kurt Preston.

"I'd say so," Juliet concurred logically.

Though it seemed to let Nielsen off the hook for the three recent lethal ligature strangulations, Lance knew the former cop was still guilty of murdering Bonnie. He also had evidence linked to other homicides in his storage unit. How? What was Nielsen's connection to Preston? Lance wondered. Were the two decades apart crimes of violence happenstance? Or had the ex-con decided to play copycat killer just for the hell of it? Lance suspected that there was something far more sinister at issue here. But what? And could they unravel the mystery surrounding Roger Nielson's death and sordid life in relation to the crimes of Kurt Preston?

"Good work," Lance commended the forensic analyst, even while knowing he had his own work cut

out for him and the HPD in bringing a serial killer
at large to justice and making the island a safe place
again.

LANCE WAS ACCOMPANIED by Gushiken as they revis-
ited the home of Nielsen's widow, Dorothy. Quite
honestly, he wasn't sure what to expect, but Lance
needed to try to connect some murderous dots to
figure out if Preston and Nielsen were somehow
related. Or if perhaps the older late detective had
passed the torch on ligature strangulation killings
to the younger man.

Gushiken, who was just as shocked, Lance knew,
at the latest turn of events in the case as he was, rang
the bell. The door opened to Dorothy, who looked
broken and seemed at a loss for words.

"Detectives Warner and Gushiken, HPD," Lance
said. "This probably isn't a good time, but we have
a few things we need to clear up in the course of the
investigation into Roger Nielsen."

"Come in," she uttered stoically, leading the way.

They stepped into the living room and Lance
spoke sympathetically, "I wish things had turned
out differently…"

"Maybe they weren't supposed to," Dorothy said
flatly. "I'm not sure what I can tell you. I never knew
anything about Roger's early life. Including his getting involved with your sister and what happened to
her. Or what he'd been up to lately. He kept it all a

big secret from me. If I'd known about any of it, I would've turned him in myself."

Lance found himself believing her. Unfortunately, what was done was done, and neither of them could rewrite the history that would forever affect both. "We have reason to believe that another person was responsible for the recent string of murders attributed to Nielsen, though the evidence and his confession to murdering Bonnie is solid."

Dorothy cocked a brow. "What other person?"

Gushiken pulled out his cell phone and brought up Preston's mug shot. "Do you recognize this man?" he asked.

She studied the photo. "Yeah. It's Kurt Preston," she identified him. "He did some carpentry work for us here at the house. He also helped Roger move some items to his storage unit. He fired Kurt after he was caught trying to steal from us." Dorothy's gaze darted from one to the other. "Are you saying he had something to do with those murders?"

Without hesitation, Lance answered solidly, "Yes. Evidence to that effect was found in your husband's storage unit that is linked to the crimes. Any idea how it may have gotten there, if Nielsen didn't put it there?"

She twisted her mouth. "Roger was always losing his keys. Someone—Kurt—could've taken them without his knowing."

Lance found this plausible but still hard to believe. "Before Nielsen fired Preston, did they hang out together?"

"If you're asking if they were friends, the answer is no," Dorothy insisted. "They may have gone out for a drink or something, but Roger's friends were closer to his own age."

"So maybe they weren't bosom buddies," Gushiken said. "That doesn't mean the two weren't partners in crime. Maybe Nielsen was grooming Preston to take his place in going after young women to strangle."

Lance added to this, in trying to come up with answers they could use in building a case against Kurt Preston, "Those three women murdered of late were killed in the same manner as the way Nielsen murdered my sister Bonnie, while using his middle name of Frank to reel her in. One of each of the recent victims' shoes and the belt used to strangle them to death were in that storage unit. They were boxed in a way that still points the finger at Nielsen in terms of being, at the very least, complicit after the fact in the murders. Unless there's something you can tell us that will shift the blame away from him, he'll go down for these homicides too even if he's innocent."

Dorothy fidgeted. "I hate what Roger did all those years ago," she voiced inexcusably. "He's had to live with it ever since. The man I knew would not have become a serial killer right under my nose. If those items were found in the storage unit, Kurt must have planted them. Don't ask me how." She sucked in a deep breath. "Now, if it's okay with you, I need to get back to making arrangements for my husband's funeral."

"We'll see ourselves out," Lance told her understandingly, while adding, "We may have further questions for you down the line, depending on how the investigation unfolds."

She nodded yieldingly and said, "Do whatever you need to do...for those girls."

A lump formed in Lance's throat as they left and he had to reconcile himself to the fact that this case wasn't over, even as he and Caroline had managed to effectively close the investigation into Bonnie's death. Her killer, Nielsen, may have been dead too, but the Belt Strangler was apparently alive and well in Kurt Preston. The perp was still a danger to women in Honolulu and needed to be apprehended as soon as possible. Weighing heavily on Lance's mind was Preston's alibi for the murder of Jill Hussey. If this held up, did Preston—and possibly Nielsen—have an accomplice? Was there even more reason to be concerned about an unsub on the loose?

Chapter Fifteen

Half an hour later, Lance was still thinking about the possibility that there may have been two present day killers, in tandem or operating independently, with three women murdered by ligature strangulation. *It's more than a little unsettling*, he mused, while driving down Nalanieha Street. The modus operandi closely mirrored the murder of Bonnie by her former lover, Roger Nielsen. Now Lance was left to figure out if the incriminating evidence discovered in his storage unit had been planted or was part of Nielsen's trophy collection as the ringleader of a band of serial killers.

He pulled up to a split-level house on Ukiuki Place in the Honolulu neighborhood of Kalihi Valley, nestled between citrus trees. Standing outside the garage was Sarah Mankiewicz, who was holding a Pomeranian dog on a leash as it did its thing in a Bird of Paradise shrub. When Lance got out of the car, Sarah came up to him.

"Detective Warner," she said warily. "I wasn't expecting to see you again."

"Neither was I," he told her. "But something's come up."

She ran her free hand nervously through loose hair. "I heard that you solved the Belt Strangler case. Did you not?"

"We thought we had." Lance glanced at the dog who was eyeing a gecko nearby, but was restrained by the leash. "Unfortunately, strong evidence now points toward Kurt Preston as the culprit in at least two of the deaths of women recently strangled by a serial killer, Sophie O'Rourke and Olivia Madekwe."

Sarah's eyes widened. "Are you sure?"

"It looks that way." Lance waited a beat. "DNA and fingerprint evidence ties Preston directly to the killings. A felony warrant has been issued for his arrest even as we speak."

"Wow." Her hand was shaking. "I have no idea where he is."

Lance had no reason to doubt this, as yet. "We think that Preston may also have killed his ex-girlfriend, Jill Hussey. Problem is, he used you as his alibi."

"Oh, that…" Sarah's voice fell an octave, giving Lance a good sense that she had lied about this. "The truth is I can't say for certain that he was at my house when Jill was killed."

"Care to explain?" Lance demanded as his brows descended over his hard gaze.

She swallowed and said thickly, "I think Kurt drugged me that night. I have no recollection of any-

thing after drinking some wine that he poured outside of my vision, till waking up the next morning.
He was there then. When I asked him about it, he
claimed that I'd simply had too much to drink." She
sighed. "I only had two glasses. Make that one and
a half. As I'd already given Kurt an alibi and wasn't
able to take it back one hundred percent, I saw no
reason to retract it, as you guys hadn't made any
further inquiries about him to make me think Kurt
might have still been a suspect."

Lance considered the date rape drug allegation,
even if it didn't involve a rape. Given Preston's previous arrest for drug possession, it made sense that
he could have spiked her drink so he could use her
as his alibi after strangling to death Jill Hussey. This
also had the dual effect of keeping Preston off the
radar as a suspect in the murders of Sophie O'Rourke
and Olivia Madekwe. But this still didn't explain to
Lance the connection between Preston and Nielsen.

He regarded Sarah. "Did Preston ever mention
anything to you about Roger Nielsen?"

"You mean the ex-cop who killed himself?" she
asked, batting her lashes.

"The same," Lance acknowledged evenly.

"Not that I can recall. When we were together,
he pretty much kept to himself about his history. Or
even what he was up to when we weren't together.
Outside of work."

"Are you saying you aren't together anymore?"

She shook her head. "After believing he drugged me, I wanted nothing more to do with Kurt."

Given the likelihood that he killed his previous girlfriend, Lance had to ask, "How did he take being dumped?"

"He didn't try to hurt me, if that's what you're asking." Sarah gripped the leash tighter as the Pomeranian sought to break free. "Just the opposite. He said he'd already moved on to someone else who caught his eye."

Lance cocked a brow, feeling that the new person in Preston's life could be in danger and needed to, at the very least, be notified that he was wanted in connection to several murders. "Did Preston happen to mention this woman's name to you?"

"Yes, he said her name was Caroline," Sarah said confidently. "Kurt seemed to relish sticking it in my face that he'd found someone prettier who was just what he was looking for in a woman."

Lance felt queasy in that moment. His instincts told him that Preston was making a beeline for Caroline, as a cold case investigator who was unsuspecting of the serial killer, to add to his ligature strangulation murders.

You've awakened this sleeping dog. Now I'm coming for you.

CAROLINE'S HEART MISSED a beat as she read the text again that someone sent her while stopped at a light en route to Lance's house. They had assumed that the earlier text messages had been sent by Roger Nielsen to try to intimidate her into dropping the cold case investigation. Now that he was dead, who was behind the latest text? Was it real? Or someone's warped idea of a practical joke, with Nielsen's crimes exposed and the perp no longer in a position to do more harm?

She glanced at the rearview mirror to see if she was being followed. There was no one there. Still, the fact that someone had threatened her and could literally be anywhere, unnerved Caroline. The last thing she needed in her life right now was to have to look over her shoulder at every turn. Especially when things seemed to be headed in the right direction between her and Lance. Or at least she sincerely hoped they were seeing eye to eye on a fresh start and a real future together, their unfortunate history notwithstanding.

Maybe I should've brought my gun with me, Caroline thought, having changed into a square neck rib knit tank top, denim shorts, and slip-on flats. She had made the decision that it wouldn't be needed for an off-duty, nonwork related outing with the man she loved. Should she go back and get her firearm, which she was legally entitled to carry at all times? Or would paranoia be playing right into the hands of whoever sent the text? Opting against returning to her condo, instead, Caroline asked the cell phone to call Lance, which it did, but it went straight to his voice mail. "Hey," she left him a message. "Just got a weird text. I'm only a couple of minutes from your place, a little ahead of schedule. If you're there, see you soon. If not, I'll pop over to the Koko Marina Center and hang out for a bit."

When she arrived, Caroline saw that the spot Lance normally parked in was empty. Was he running late? Though early herself, she wondered if she should wait. Or stick to the game plan. Rather than believe that she was being stood up by him like before when they started to get too close, Caroline gave Lance the benefit of the doubt that he was as ready and willing as her to take the next step in their relationship. Probably tying up loose ends of the Belt Strangler case, with Roger Nielsen no longer able to terrorize women in Honolulu or anywhere else on the island of Oahu, for that matter.

I'm sure I can keep myself busy till he comes home, Caroline thought, as she opted to drive over to the shopping center on Kalanianaole Highway. Once there, she parked and made her way around, checking out some of the specialty stores, boutiques, and gift shops, as well as beauty and health locations, while imagining that she was overdue for a good professional massage and getting her nails done. She would make the time to do just that.

Taking out her cell phone, which was ringing, Caroline suspected it was Lance calling to apologize for missing her, but letting her know he was home now and ready to greet her upon her arrival. She gushed at the thought. Only before she could answer, Caroline felt something press hard against the center of her back. Then a deep voice said, "I wouldn't answer that, if I were you. Otherwise, I just might have to shoot you on the spot, Detective Yashima."

"Pick up," Lance urged Caroline as he phoned her, while pacing inside his house. He waited but there was no answer. Seconds earlier, he had listened to her voice mail, informing him that she was headed there, but would go to the Koko Marina Center if he wasn't home yet. He'd just arrived, hoping she had waited. But with no sign of her car, he had to assume she went to the shopping center. That did little to lessen his concern, knowing that Kurt Preston was going after Caroline and she needed to be warned. What if it was too late? Did she have her gun with her? The notion of the serial killer laying even one hand on the love of his life infuriated Lance. Having lost his big sister to violence, he couldn't lose Caroline too.

He sent her a text, identifying Preston as the Belt Strangler, while telling her to be on guard, in spite of the BOLO issued for the murder suspect and his Infiniti QX50. With no response, Lance tried calling again, but no response. It was as if Caroline's phone had suddenly gone dead, causing him further anxiety. *Maybe I should head to the Koko Marina Cen-*

ter and see if I can locate her, he told himself with a sense of desperation.

When his cell phone rang suddenly, Lance's hopes that it was Caroline were dashed as Hugo Gushiken appeared in the video chat. "I've got news," he began bleakly. "Preston's vehicle was just spotted leaving the Koko Marina Center."

Lance felt a lump in his throat. "Caroline went there." Had the perp abducted her?

"In the darkness, there's no indication he's accompanied by anyone," Gushiken said. "And it looks like Preston may be headed toward Koko Head District Park."

His gut told Lance that the serial killer had abducted Caroline and planned to add her to his victims, in a location that would give him time to kill her and make a clean getaway. "I want all available officers after this guy," Lance ordered. "If he has Caroline, he could use her as a hostage, if all else fails. Or worse."

"I'm on it," the detective insisted. "Let's not get ahead of ourselves, as far as Caroline is concerned, assuming she has been taken by him. From what I've heard about her from a friend in the Attorney General's office, she knows a thing or two about martial arts and won't make it easy for him, if Preston were ever to lower his guard. He can only go so far, now that we're onto him."

"I'm headed out," Lance told him, knowing that every second counted till he found Caroline. Privy to her practicing Lua, he didn't doubt that she was capable of defending herself in whatever means were at her disposal. But he also knew that the man who now seemed to be fixated on her, had murdered three other women and was in no way to be taken lightly in setting his deadly sights on Caroline.

To HER DISMAY, Caroline found herself being forced behind the wheel of her kidnapper's SUV at gunpoint and told to drive to Koko Head District Park. When he had identified himself as Kurt Preston, she played dumb, forcing him to admit to being the ex-boyfriend of Jill Hussey, the first of three women strangled to death by the Belt Strangler. Caroline had thought Roger Nielsen to be the serial killer, as an add-on to the ligature strangulation of Bonnie Warner, before taking his own life. Could they have been deliberately misdirected by the true killer?

"I'm sure the suspense is killing you, Detective Caroline Yashima," Preston said from the passenger seat, while pointing what looked to be a .357 Magnum revolver at her. "All right, I'll get to the nitty-gritty. For starters, yeah, it was me who sent you the text messages, in case you hadn't figured out that much. Had to make you think it was Nielsen behind the texts."

"But why?" Caroline asked, as the headlights cut through the darkness. She was admittedly thrown off that Nielsen wasn't guilty of sending the intimidating text messages after all. She also needed to get as much out of her abductor as possible, knowing that Lance was likely aware of her absence and probably already searching for her. She suspected he was knowledgeable on what Preston had been up to and had planned for her, which couldn't be good. Unfortunately, she had lost her ability to communicate with Lance and warn him about any of this, as the perp had snatched Caroline's phone from her and smashed it with his foot, making it inoperable.

"That one is easy," Preston said with a chuckle. "It was all part of my master plan in using what Nielsen had already done in killing that coed twenty years ago as both payback and to chart my own course in picking up where he left off. Only be better at it. You see, I was hired by him to work on some flooring at his house and help move some things into his storage facility. When we had a falling out and he canned me without paying for my services, while threatening to press charges for stealing from him, I broke into the unit and discovered something very interesting. Turned out that Nielsen kept a journal hidden in there in which he confessed to the murder of Bonnie Warner as the result of some lovesick obsession. He even mentioned hanging onto one of her shoes and the belt used to strangle her to death, as a stark reminder of the good old days. Can you imagine that?"

Actually, Caroline could imagine that for someone as driven, egotistical and confident enough to believe he would get away with it as Roger Nielsen apparently had been. They hadn't found the journal, which when the handwriting had been analyzed and verified, would have only further added to Nielsen's guilt, along with the other incriminating evidence.

"I took the journal," Preston read her mind, "so I could study what made a killer tick and use it to my advantage." He stopped abruptly while they were on Kaumakani Street and directed her to drive into the park and into a parking lot near the baseball diamond. "We'll pick this up once we start to get where we're going. She watched as he grabbed a headlamp from the back seat and put it on. "Get out," he ordered, aiming the gun at her, forcing her to comply.

"Where are you taking me?" Caroline demanded, while realizing she wasn't exactly in any position to challenge his authority, as long as he was the one holding the weapon. *Doesn't mean I won't look for an avenue of escape*, she thought. *Not to mention, a way to stay alive.*

"Oh, you'll see." Preston laughed wryly. "Just somewhere that we won't be disturbed, till I'm finished with you. Then I'll be on my way. Don't worry about it."

He plans to kill me, Caroline told herself with dread. Not that this came as a complete shock. He obviously wanted to get some awful things off his chest and make sure she never told a soul. She considered some other things he might try to do to her, were she unable to fight him off.

As they started walking, guided only by the illumination from the headlamp, it dawned on Caroline that they were headed toward the Koko Head Trail. The 1.4-mile trail's pathway consisted of 1,048 railway ties constructed by the military for transporting soldiers and supplies during World War II, and since abandoned, that led to a steep incline to the Koko Head Crater summit. She and Lance had once taken the arduous journey as an adventure and test of fitness, both passing with flying colors. But she had been more dressed for the part than now. And her hair was loose instead of tied up. Whereas, her kidnapper had clearly planned this in advance, wearing a slub tee, hiking shorts, and running sneakers. Not to mention the handgun he was carrying. She could only wonder why he had chosen to target her as the next victim of what she assumed to be the real Belt Strangler.

With Caroline being forced to walk precariously on the stairs ahead of him, Preston said, "I have to admit, I hadn't really thought of killing Jill till Nielsen implanted the thought. He made it look so easy to strangle someone with a leather belt and get away with it. Jill was a real bitch at times and needed to go after turning her back on me. I drugged Sarah and used her as my alibi, while slipping out of her bed and strangling Jill. You should've seen the look on her face as she was dying, knowing there wasn't a thing she could do about it but watch it happen."

What a psychopath, Caroline thought. How could they have missed this? But wasn't that precisely how killers became serial killers—by being just cunning enough to fool the cops? "Why the others?" She decided to feed his ego in buying more time to survive this nightmare.

"I wanted to do Roger the Dodger one better... two...three..." Preston laughed. "Knowing about the cold case you and the brother of Nielsen's victim, Detective Warner, were reopening, I figured why not make them believe that Bonnie Warner's killer had resurfaced and was at it again? I knew Nielsen wasn't exactly in a position to come forward and admit his innocence without incriminating himself in the murder twenty years ago. So, I set him up to take the fall while I carried on the crimes on his behalf, so to speak."

Caroline had to believe that Lance and the HPD were onto Preston, even if the Belt Strangler case had appeared to be put to rest. But what if they weren't? What if Lance believed her absence had been explained by the voice mail and that he had nothing to worry about? Or a serial killer still to catch?

She stopped and faced the killer, who had kept just enough distance between them to keep her from trying to grab his gun. "If you hope to make this stick with Roger Nielsen being the Belt Strangler,

killing me will only make Detective Warner and
other investigators suspicious," Caroline told him.
"Why not quit while you're ahead?"

"Where would the fun be in that?" Preston chuckled sardonically. "As for keeping the authorities off
my back and convinced that they have their serial
killer in Nielsen, you and I are about to start a whole
new tradition." He made the headlamp brighter so
she could see more of him. "Do you see a leather belt
anywhere? I don't." Another laugh came out of him,
before his features contorted and he barked, "Now
get moving again, or I swear I'll put a bullet in your
head right here and now. With what I have planned
for you, at least you'll have a fighting chance. Or
maybe not."

Caroline did as he demanded and started to walk
toward the summit, while wondering what he considered a fighting chance. Shooting her and leaving
her to bleed out while hoping for a miracle to survive? Challenging her to a fist fight? Leaving her to
find her way back in the dark? Or did he have something else planned that would put her life on the line?

LANCE SPOTTED PRESTON's blue Infiniti QX50 in the
parking area of the Koko Head District Park that was
close to the baseball field. Approaching the vehicle
carefully, his weapon drawn, Lance saw that there
was no one inside. Shining his flashlight through the
back side window, he saw what looked to be Caro-

line's leather hobo bag tossed onto the seat. *She is in Preston's clutches*, Lance thought, his pulse racing with apprehension. Why had he brought her to this park, in particular? Was she even still alive at this point?

Lance had to believe Caroline was alive and kicking against a dangerous adversary. *Have to get to her and stop him*, he mused. As law enforcement fanned out in search of the serial killer suspect, it hit Lance that he was standing steps from the entrance to the Koko Crater Trail. He and Caroline had gone up once to the Koko Head Crater summit and challenged each other every step of the way. Preston must have taken her there, planning to force her off the pathway, one way or another, to a tragic death. *I won't let that happen*, Lance told himself, more determined than he could ever remember, with his and Caroline's future hanging in the balance.

Bringing with him a couple of armed and well-conditioned officers who looked to match his own fitness, Lance headed up the trail, having already put on the lace-up sneakers he kept in his car. Otherwise, he was comfortably dressed for the trek in a camp shirt and athletic fit jeans. Already, Lance found himself imagining what he would say to Caroline once this nightmare was over, knowing to think otherwise would be laying down to defeat. That wasn't in the cards for either for them. Instead, he focused on making her listen and not taking no for an answer to his love and the building of a life together.

"STOP!" PRESTON'S VOICE shattered the quiet, with them halfway up the summit, atop a railway bridge. Even in the darkness, Caroline remembered that there was a ravine below. "I'm afraid it's the end of the line," he said wickedly, pointing the revolver. "At least for you. Cold case detective becomes a cold case herself." He chuckled. "Kind of poetic, don't you think? Now jump!"

Reaching her limit on being a victim and with no other cards to play when dealing with a serial killer sociopath, Caroline's instincts for survival kicked in. The Lua martial art she had learned as a child was her ace in the hole and one he would never see coming. She realized that Preston had come right up to her, either planning to shoot point-blank or force her off the bridge and into the ravine. She opted for neither and, with lightning speed, grabbed hold of the gun's barrel, pushing it away from her face as a shot went off. Just as quickly, Caroline locked onto the wrist of his gun hand, and began manipulating the pressure points, twisting sharply, till she heard the snap of the bone.

Preston howled like a rabid animal and the weapon fell from his hand. He came at her and Caroline raised her foot and slammed it at just the right angle as hard as she could into the side of his knee, badly dislocating it. Her attacker cried out again, losing his balance. She hit him squarely at the base of the neck, causing Preston to gasp for air. Believing this was enough to make her getaway, Caroline whisked past him, intending to run down the stairs. But he managed to grab her from behind and shoved, so she fell onto the railway ties.

As she tried to crawl to grab the gun nearby, Caroline prepared to do battle with everything she had should she fail. She managed to lift the firearm, but Preston was already charging at her like a man possessed. He reached her before she could turn the gun onto him, operating on one gimpy leg, but determined to see this through. Then Caroline heard a shot ring out, hitting Preston, who was stopped dead in his tracks. Another shot pierced his chest, then he backpedaled till he fell off the bridge and into the ravine.

While assessing what just happened, she scrambled to her feet in time to see Lance moving toward her with a flashlight and firearm. He put the gun back in its holster and wrapped protective arms around her and gave her a passionate kiss, which she gladly returned with equal ardor before their lips parted.

"It's over," he said quietly, followed by, "Are you hurt?"

"Other than a few scrapes and bruises, I think I'll live," she assured him. "How did you find me?"

"To make a long story short, forensic evidence fingered Kurt Preston as the killer of Sophie O'Rourke and Olivia Madekwe. When I questioned his ex-girlfriend, Sarah Mankiewicz, she believed Preston had drugged her when they were supposed to be together at the time Jill Hussey was killed—meaning his alibi fell apart for that murder." Lance held her a little closer and Caroline almost wished they could stay that way forever. "According to Sarah, Preston had claimed to have a new girlfriend named Caroline. Something told me that person in his warped mind was you."

She shuddered to think that he had been stalking her, waiting for the right moment to nab her and carry out his maniacal plan. What if he had been successful? How many more women would have died?

"A warrant was issued for Preston's arrest," Lance continued, "and when his car was spotted driving away from Koko Marina Center and heading toward Koko Head District Park, I was all but certain he had abducted you. That was cinched when I spotted your handbag in the back of his car."

Caroline nodded satisfyingly. "I was hoping that wouldn't escape your notice."

"Not where it concerned you." Lance pulled them apart. "I figured that Preston took you up the Koko Head Trail, planning to kill you and keep us guessing. I wasn't about to let that happen."

"Neither was I," she uttered. "Too much to live for." *You for one*, Caroline mused.

"You can say that again." His voice cracked, telling her they were on the same track, no pun intended.

"Preston confessed to killing the three women and setting up Roger Nielsen to take the rap by breaking into his storage unit and planting the incriminating evidence," Caroline informed him, to further establish Preston's guilt as the Belt Strangler. "He also said he stole Nielsen's journal, which outlined his own guilt in killing Bonnie, and used it against him while inspiring Preston to forge his own path as a serial killer."

"Crazy," Lance muttered disbelievingly.

"Which one?" she asked wryly.

"Both Nielsen and Preston. Two homicidal peas in a pod."

She giggled. "Can't argue with you there."

"Didn't think so." Lance chuckled. "Let's get off these railway stairs."

Caroline initiated a short kiss, as a prelude to things to come, and said eagerly, "I think that's an excellent idea."

Epilogue

With Roger Nielsen and Kurt Preston both dead, the latter succumbing to the injuries sustained from the fall and being shot, closing two murder investigations at once, Lance finally felt he had some leeway in putting all his cards on the table. After a near miss, he wasn't about to let Caroline slip away. Not again. Not ever. Now came the hard part. Convincing her of his sincerity. Or had she already decided that he wasn't going anywhere. But would go everywhere, as long as she was by his side?

As they sipped red wine on the vintage leather couch in Lance's living room after the ordeal Caroline had been put through, he knew it was long overdue to do right by her. He took a breath and waited for their eyes to lock, before saying, "If the recent experiences we've both been put through, including having to relive Bonnie's death, have taught me anything, it's that I don't want to wait till tomorrow to do what I can do today. Especially when tomorrow may never come."

She batted her eyes with anticipation. "What exactly are you saying?" she put him on the spot.

"I'm saying that I want to spend the rest of my life trying to make you happy, as husband and wife."

Caroline tasted the wine. "Are you sure this is what you want?" Doubt danced in her pretty eyes.

"I've never been surer of anything in my life," Lanced insisted. "I know I screwed up when we were together before and I've had to live with that. But I was going through some things that clouded my judgment. That's over and done with. I won't make that mistake again. If you give me a chance, I'll make sure you never regret it." He took her trembling hand. "I'm in love with you, Caroline, and have known that for a long time, even if I turned my back on that love. I'm asking you now to marry me and give us the opportunity to live the life we were meant to."

"Yes, yes, I'll marry you, Lance Warner," she uttered in a bubbly voice and kissed him. "It might not have been love at first sight, but I pretty much knew early on in our first date that this was a gorgeous man that I wanted to spend the rest of my life with." She sipped her wine. "I'm just so happy that you finally caught up with me and we both want the same things moving forward."

Lance laughed and they kissed again. He thought about having children, grandchildren, making a strong effort to smell the roses in life through relaxation, travel, and making each second count. Basically, everything they had talked about in having a life together. "Admittedly, I can be slow at times," he said guiltily. "But I'm more than ready to make up for it."

Caroline chuckled. "I'll hold you to that."

"You better." He grinned sideways before becoming serious. *This is the moment I've been waiting for practically my entire life*, he told himself. Removing something from the pocket of his jeans, Lance held up a one carat 14K white gold split shank engagement ring with an oval cut diamond. "This was my grandmother's ring. She passed it to my mother. It was her intention to give it to Bonnie when she became engaged." He choked up. "My sister never got that opportunity, so I inherited the ring. It belongs to you, Caroline," he told her. "The love of my life."

Lance slid it on her finger. It was a perfect fit. He watched as her eyes welled up with happy, poignant tears. "Mahalo," she uttered. "I'll treasure it forever."

"I know you will. Just as I'll treasure you forever, Caroline."

They kissed again fervently, to seal the deal.

SIX MONTHS LATER, Caroline and Lance were married and living at their marina front home. Having decided to keep the Waikiki condominium as a rental property, they occasionally used it for a romantic weekend getaway. Both were incredibly busy with their careers, with Caroline diving into new cold case investigations with all the usual twists, turns and the unexpected. Meanwhile, Lance was dedicated to solving current day homicides on Oahu, while occasionally lending Caroline a helping hand whenever their cases crossed paths. She found no room for complaint. Especially with a little one on the way, promising to fill their hearts and souls with untold joy and sleepless nights. As far as she was concerned, Caroline believed that she had the best of all worlds, beginning with the best husband a woman could ever have. The fact that he never allowed her to forget how lucky he was in having her as his wife, made their union all the more special and apropos in the spirit of Hawaii.

They stood on the lanai with friends, Rachelle Compagno and her boyfriend, Harold Horikoshi— a Hawaiian hunk with black hair in a two-block cut, who was as tall and fit as Lance was—whom Rachelle was madly in love with. Caroline expected them to announce their own engagement at any time. She was happy for her friend, just as she knew Rachelle had her back.

While Lance was hovering over his pellet grill and smoker, tending to steaks and burgers with assistance from Harold, Caroline sipped iced tea with Rachelle, as they took in the spectacular views on a clear day of the Koko Marina, Koolau Range, and Koko Crater. Cringing at the thought of Kurt Preston forcing her at gunpoint to climb up the Koko Crater

Trail, then nearly pushing her into the ravine, gave Caroline goose bumps. *He very nearly ended my life and the joy of becoming Lance's wife and partner,* she told herself. But Preston had failed, she needed to be reminded. Evil lost out to goodness and tenacious police work. So too had Roger Nielsen. He may have taken away Bonnie's life, full of so much potential, twenty years ago, but he had not taken away her spirit. And Lance had never given up on solving his sister's murder. Caroline was just happy to be a part of giving her husband back that part of him that he kept bottled up so long as Bonnie's death remained unsolved.

Rachelle made a face. "Please don't tell me you're thinking about that creep who made you go up the trail."

Caroline smiled gently. "No," she told a little white lie. "Just taking it all in."

"Good. The last thing you want is a dead man to hold power over you. You took everything that serial killer could throw at you and triumphed. That's something worth celebrating every day."

"I couldn't agree more," Caroline told her, promising herself not to dwell on the past and perps like Preston and Nielsen, who didn't deserve her attention after the fact. "Why don't we go see how the guys are coming along with the food."

"Excellent idea" Rachelle said.

When Caroline walked up to Lance, he said teasingly, "Can't stand to be away from me, huh?"

Her eyes crinkled. "What do you think?"

"I think it's more the other way around." He hit her with a devilish grin. "I know it is. You have that kind of effect on me, Caroline. Or haven't you already guessed that?"

"Yes, I have guessed," she said, coloring. "Especially since it works both ways." She tilted her chin and planted a long kiss on his mouth.

"I believe you." Lance laughed, licking his lips. "Hey, Harold, what do you say we give these two a little privacy?"

"Do we have to?" He faked being wounded at the mere suggestion. "Just when things were starting to get interesting."

"Yes," Rachelle told him with a laugh. "Can't you see that they have some serious vibes going on? Just like us."

Harold chuckled. "I get it. Let's go inside and refresh the beverages."

"Done." She grabbed his hand and they walked off.

Caroline beamed at Lance and said sweetly, "Now, where were we?"

"Just getting started," he declared, resuming the kiss.

* * * * *

#2127 CONARD COUNTY: K-9 DETECTIVES
Conard County: The Next Generation • by Rachel Lee

Veterans Jenna Blair and Kell McLaren have little in common. But when they join forces to solve a local murder with the help of Kell's K-9 companion, they uncover a web of danger that requires them to reevaluate their partnership...and their growing feelings for one another.

#2128 ONE NIGHT STANDOFF
Covert Cowboy Soldiers • by Nicole Helm

When Hazeleigh Hart finds her boss's murdered body, she runs...directly into rancher Landon Thompson. He vows to help clear her name—he knows she's no murderess. But will their hideout be discovered by the killer before Hazeleigh is exonerated?

#2129 TEXAS BODYGUARD: LUKE
San Antonio Security • by Janie Crouch

Claire Wallace has stumbled upon corporate espionage—and murder. Now the software engineer is being framed for both crimes. Security expert Luke Patterson protected her in the past and he'll risk it all to do it again. But is the real culprit already one step ahead of them?

#2130 DANGER ON MAUI
Hawaii CI • by R. Barri Flowers

Murders, stalkers and serial killers! It's all fair game in the world of true crime writer Daphne Dockery. But when life imitates art, she'll need Hawaiian homicide detective Kenneth Kealoha to protect her from becoming the next victim in her repertoire.

#2131 FRENCH QUARTER FATALE
by Joanna Wayne

FBI terrorist special agent Keenan Carter knows nothing about being a famous actress's daughter. That doesn't diminish his attraction to Josette Guillory...or his determination to protect her from the assassin targeting her for her inheritance. If only they could locate her missing mother to get to the truth...

#2132 GOING ROGUE IN RED RYE COUNTY
Secure One • by Katie Mettner

Dirty cops sabotaged FBI Agent Mini August's latest operation and left her on the run for her life. But when Special Agent Roman Jacobs finds his injured, compromised ex-partner in a North Dakota forest, will he risk his badge to help her...or finish the job her target started?

HARLEQUIN
PLUS

Try the best multimedia subscription service for romance readers like you!

Read, Watch and Play.

Experience the easiest way to get the romance content you crave.

Start your **FREE TRIAL** at
<u>www.harlequinplus.com/freetrial</u>.